4

Short Stories of
O. Henry
歐・亨利短篇小說

Original Author	O. Henry
Adaptors	Brian J. Stuart
Illustrator	Kim Hyeon-jeong

WORDS
800

MP3

Let's Enjoy Masterpieces!

All the beautiful fairy tales and masterpieces that you have encountered during your childhood remain as warm memories in your adulthood. This time, let's indulge in the world of masterpieces through English. You can enjoy the depth and beauty of original works, which you can't enjoy through Chinese translations.

The stories are easy for you to understand because of your familiarity with them. When you enjoy reading, your ability to understand English will also rapidly improve.

This series of *Let's Enjoy Masterpieces* is a special reading comprehension booster program, devised to improve reading comprehension for beginners whose command of English is not satisfactory, or who are elementary, middle, and high school students. With this program, you can enjoy reading masterpieces in English with fun and efficiency.

This carefully planned program is composed of 5 levels, from the beginner level of 350 words to the intermediate and advanced levels of 1,000 words. With this program's level-by-level system, you are able to read famous texts in English and to savor the true pleasure of the world's language.

The program is well conceived, composed of reader-friendly explanations of English expressions and grammar, quizzes to help the student learn vocabulary and understand the meaning of the texts, and fabulous illustrations that adorn every page. In addition, with our "Guide to Listening," not only is reading comprehension enhanced but also listening comprehension skills are highlighted.

In the audio recording of the book, texts are vividly read by professional American voice actors. The texts are rewritten, according to the levels of the readers by an expert editorial staff of native speakers, on the basis of standard American English with the ministry of education recommended vocabulary. Therefore, it will be of great help even for all the students that want to learn English.

Please indulge yourself in the fun of reading and listening to English through *Let's Enjoy Masterpieces*.

歐·亨利

William S. Porter
(O. Henry)
(1862–1910)

O. Henry was an American short-story writer and a master of surprise endings. The well-known name of O. Henry was William Sidney Porter's pseudonym, and according to some people, it was also his cat's name.

William S. Porter was born in Greensboro, North Carolina. His father, Algernon Sidney Porter, was a physician. When William was three, his mother died from tuberculosis, and he and his father moved to the home of his paternal grandmother.

William was an avid reader; however, at the age of fifteen he left school and then worked as a bookkeeper in his uncle's drugstore. He took a number of different jobs over the next several years, including pharmacist, draftsman, journalist, and clerk. In 1896, he was convicted of embezzling money and was sentenced to five years in prison. He was released on July 24, 1901 for good behavior after serving three years.

While in prison, he started to write short stories based on his own experiences. Not wanting his readers to know he was in prison, he started using the penname "O. Henry." He moved to New York after being released from prison and earnestly began to write. In New York, he wrote almost 300 short stories in 10 years.

His well-known *The Last Leaf* and *The Gift of the Magi* and other sensitive stories mainly describe the joys and sorrows of the common people and the poor living in the back streets of New York and the Southern parts of the United States.

O. Henry wrote with humor, wit, and pathos and showed his deep insight into human psychology and feelings. His clever conceptions, artful plots, and surprising endings also show his talents and abundant imagination as an author.

The Last Leaf

The setting of the story "The Last Leaf" is Greenwich Village, New York, 1905. The lively opening scene introduces the reader to Johnsy, a painter, and her new roommate Sue, a sculptor. The two young female artists share an apartment. As the winter approaches and the weather gets colder, Johnsy becomes ill with pneumonia. Despite Sue's constant nursing, Johnsy is not getting any better. She is near death and loses her hope in living. She lies in bed, staring through the window at an ivy vine on the brick wall. She believes that she will die by the time the last leaf falls from the vine.

However, an unexpected hero arrives to save Johnsy. The elderly Mr. Behrman is an unsuccessful artist and their neighbor. He wants to restore to the dying Johnsy the will to live. Struggling with his own health problems, he defies a stormy night to paint a leaf on the outdoor vine—a leaf that will never fall. Cold and wet from painting in the rain, he catches pneumonia and dies. However, that leaf gives Johnsy enough hope to survive her illness, and it also creates the masterpiece Mr. Behrman always dreamed of painting.

The Cop and the Anthem

"The Cop and the Anthem" shows in ironic ways how Mr. Timothy J. Bowers, a goodhearted homeless man, goes to jail. As the season becomes colder and colder, Mr. Timothy J. Bowers, worried about the coming winter, decides that his best course of action is to get himself arrested. He thinks jail-time would guarantee him a warm place to sleep.

After Twenty Years

"After Twenty Years" tells about two friends, Bob and Jimmy, who made an appointment to meet each other again "after twenty years" in the same place and at the same time they dinned the night before they parted. They thought by then they ought to have their destinies worked out and their fortunes made. Bob, who has great success in the West, comes back to the meeting place to wait for Jimmy.

HOW TO USE THIS BOOK
本書使用說明

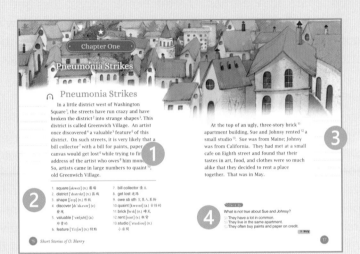

① Original English texts

It is easy to understand the meaning of the text, because the text is rewritten according to the levels of the readers.

② Explanation of the vocabulary

The words and expressions that include vocabulary above the elementary level are clearly defined.

③ Response notes

Spaces are included in the book so you can take notes about what you don't understand or what you want to remember.

④ Check UP

Review quizzes to check your understanding of the text.

🎧 Audio Recording

In the audio recording, native speakers narrate the texts in standard American English. By combining the written words and the audio recording, you can listen to English with great ease.

Audio books have been popular in Britain and America for many decades. They allow the listener to experience the proper word pronunciation and sentence intonation that add important meaning and drama to spoken English. Students will benefit from listening to the recording twenty or more times.

After you are familiar with the text and recording, listen once more with your eyes closed to check your listening comprehension. Finally, after you can listen with your eyes closed and understand every word and every sentence, you are then ready to mimic the native speaker.

Then you should make a recording by reading the text yourself. Then play both recordings to compare your oral skills with those of a native speaker.

HOW TO IMPROVE READING ABILITY
如何增進英文閱讀能力

1 *Catch key words*

Read the key words in the sentences and practice catching the gist of the meaning of the sentence. You might question how working with a few important words could enhance your reading ability. However, it's quite effective. If you continue to use this method, you will find out that the key words and your knowledge of people and situations enables you to understand the sentence.

2 *Divide long sentences*

Read in chunks of meaning, dividing sentences into meaningful chunks of information. In the book, chunks are arranged in sentences according to meaning. If you consider the sentences backwards or grammatically, your reading speed will be slow and you will find it difficult to listen to English.

You are ready to move to a more sophisticated level of comprehension when you find that narrowly focusing on chunks is irritating. Instead of considering the chunks, you will make it a habit to read the sentence from the beginning to the end to figure out the meaning of the whole.

③ Make inferences and assumptions

Making inferences and assumptions is part of your ability. If you don't know, try to guess the meaning of the words. Although you don't know all the words in context, don't go straight to the dictionary. Developing an ability to make inferences in the context is important.

The first way to figure out the meaning of a word is from its context. If you cannot make head or tail out of the meaning of a word, look at what comes before or after it. Ask yourself what can happen in such a situation. Make your best guess as to the word's meaning. Then check the explanations of the word in the book or look up the word in a dictionary.

④ Read a lot and reread the same book many times

There is no shortcut to mastering English. Only if you do a lot of reading will you make your way to the summit. Read fun and easy books with an average of less than one new word per page. Try to immerse yourself in English as often as you can.

Spend time "swimming" in English. Language learning research has shown that immersing yourself in English will help you improve your English, even though you may not be aware of what you're learning.

CONTENTS

Before You Read

Sue

I'm just a poor artist living with my best friend Johnsy. It's getting really cold, and Johnsy has come down with[1] pneumonia[2]. The doctor doesn't give Johnsy much hope of surviving[3]. This breaks my heart!

1. come down with 染病   2. pneumonia [njuːˋmoʊnɪə] (n.) 肺炎
3. survive [sərˋvaɪv] (v.) 存活下來

Johnsy

I feel so sick and I'm tired. I know I will die soon. I just want to hold on[4] until the last leaf of the ivy[5] branch falls. Soon the last leaf will fall[6], and I too will die.

4. hold on 堅持下去；撐住   5. ivy [ˋaɪvi] (n.) 長春藤
6. fall [fɔːl] (v.) 掉落

Behrman

What is this nonsense[7]? The little girl thinks she will die when a leaf falls from a vine? This is crazy! I must do something to protect[8] the poor little thing.

7. nonsense [ˋnɑːnsens] (n.) 胡說八道；無稽之談
8. protect [prəˋtekt] (v.) 保護

Short Stories of O. Henry

Soapy

Burr. . . I guess it's time for me to arrange my annual winter trip to the Island[9]. No, no, it's not an island in the Caribbean. It's the Island near New York City where the prison[10] is. I just have to figure out[11] how to get there.

9. island [`aɪlənd] (n.) 島嶼   10. prison [`prɪzən] (n.) 監獄
11. figure out 想出辦法

Jimmy

Twenty years! That's how long it's been since I last saw my childhood friend. But tonight, we will meet again. That's right, we made an appointment[12] to meet at the very restaurant where we parted[13] ways 20 years ago. It's a hardware store[14] now. Wait, there's someone at the doorway[15].

12. make an appointment 有約   13. part [pɑːrt] (v.) 分開；告別
14. hardware store 五金行   15. doorway [`dɔːrweɪ] (n.) 門口；出入口

Bob

Hey there. Do you know a guy named Jimmy Wells? I'm supposed to[16] meet him right here, at 10 o'clock p.m. I wonder if Jimmy changed. I certainly have changed a bit myself. And I did pretty well.

16. be supposed to 應該

The Last Leaf

最後一片葉子

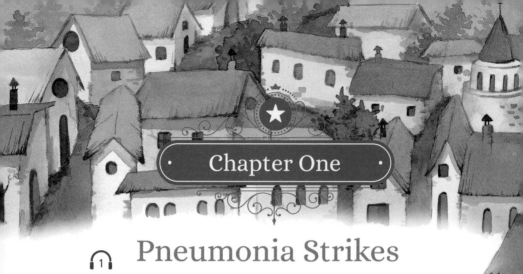

Chapter One

Pneumonia Strikes

In a little district west of Washington Square[1], the streets have run crazy and have broken the district[2] into strange shapes[3]. This district is called Greenwich Village. An artist once discovered[4] a valuable[5] feature[6] of this district. On such streets, it is very likely that a bill collector[7] with a bill for paints, paper, and canvas would get lost[8] while trying to find the address of the artist who owes[9] him money! So, artists came in large numbers to quaint[10], old Greenwich Village.

---

1. square [skwer] (n.) 廣場
2. district [`dɪstrɪkt] (n.) 區域
3. shape [ʃeɪp] (n.) 形狀
4. discover [dɪ`skʌvər] (v.) 發現
5. valuable [`væljubl] (a.) 珍貴的
6. feature [`fi:tʃər] (n.) 特點
7. bill collector 債主
8. get lost 迷路
9. owe sb sth 欠某人某物
10. quaint [kweɪnt] (a.) 古怪的
11. brick [brɪk] (n.) 磚瓦
12. rent [rent] (v.) 租貸
13. studio [`stu:dioʊ] (n.) 小房間

At the top of an ugly, three-story brick[11] apartment building, Sue and Johnsy rented[12] a small studio[13]. Sue was from Maine; Johnsy was from California. They had met at a small cafe on Eighth street and found that their tastes in art, food, and clothes were so much alike that they decided to rent a place together. That was in May.

 Check Up

What is not true about Sue and Johnsy?

a They have a lot in common.
b They live in the same apartment.
c They often buy paints and paper on credit.

Ans: c

In November, a cold, unseen[1] stranger whom the doctors called pneumonia came to Greenwich Village, touching people here and there with his icy[2] fingers. A small woman with blood thinned[3] by the warm California sun was no match for[4] the tough[5] and deadly[6] illness[7]. Johnsy got pneumonia, and it made her very ill. She lay, hardly moving on her iron-framed bed, looking through the small

window at the brick wall of the building next door.

One morning, the busy doctor invited Sue into the hallway[8]. His eyes were sad under his bushy[9] gray eyebrows.

1. unseen [ʌnˋsiːn] (a.) 看不見的；隱形的
2. icy [ˋaɪsi] (a.) 冰冷的
3. thin [θɪn] (v.) 使變瘦
4. match for 敵得過；比得上
5. tough [tʌf] (a.) 棘手的；難纏的
6. deadly [ˋdɛdli] (a.) 致死的
7. illness [ˋɪlnɪs] (n.) 病痛
8. hallway [ˋhɔːlˏweɪ] (n.) 走道
9. bushy [ˋbuʃi] (a.) 濃密的
10. clinical thermometer 診療用溫度計
11. depend on 取決於
12. will [wɪl] (n.) 意願；意志
13. give up 放棄
14. matter [ˋmætər] (v.) 有關係
15. medicine [ˋmedɪsən] (n.) 藥品
16. get well 病癒

"She has one chance in — let us say, ten," he said, as he looked at his clinical thermometer[10]. "And that chance depends on[11] her will[12] to live. Some-times when people give up[13] trying to live, it doesn't matter[14] what medicines[15] I give. Your friend has decided, for some reason, that she is not going to get well[16]."

 Check Up

What's no match for pheumonia?

- [a] The deadly illness
- [b] The California sun
- [c] A cold, unseen stranger

Ans: b

19

"Is she worried about anything?" continued the doctor.

"She . . . she wanted to paint[1] the Bay of Naples[2] someday," said Sue.

"Paint? Nonsense! Does she have any important worries[3], like about a man, for instance[4]?"

"A man?" asked Sue, with a touch of[5] sarcasm[6] in her voice. "Is a man worth[7] dying for? But, no, doctor; there is nothing of the kind."

"Well, she is weak," said the doctor. "I will do all that science, as I understand it, can accomplish[8]. But whenever my patient[9] begins to count[10] the days until her own funeral[11], I subtract[12] 50 percent from the power of medicine to cure. If you could get her to ask one question about the new winter clothing styles, I will promise you a one-in-five chance for her, instead of one in ten."

1. paint [peɪnt] (v.) 繪畫
2. the Bay of Naples 那不勒斯港（位於義大利南部）
3. worry [ˋwɜːri] (n.) 憂慮
4. for instance 例如
5. a touch of 些許
6. sarcasm [ˋsɑːrkæzəm] (n.) 嘲諷
7. be worth v-ing 值得……
8. accomplish [əˋkɑːmplɪʃ] (v.) 達成
9. patient [ˋpeɪʃənt] (n.) 病患
10. count [kaʊnt] (v.) 計算
11. funeral [ˋfjuːnərəl] (n.) 葬禮
12. subtract [səbˋtrækt] (v.) 減去

After the doctor had gone, Sue went into the workroom[13] and cried her eyes dry[14]. Then she walked carelessly into Johnsy's room with her drawing board[15], whistling[16] a popular and lively tune[17].

✓ *Check Up*

The chance for Johnsy to get well at present is _____ in _____.

13. workroom [ˋwɜ:rkrʊm] (n.)
    工作室
14. cry one's eye dry
    把眼淚都哭乾了
15. drawing board 畫板
16. whistle [ˋwɪsəl] (v.) 吹口哨
17. tune [tuːn] (n.) 曲調

Johnsy lay, scarcely[1] making a move[2] under the bedsheets[3], with her face toward the window. Sue stopped whistling, thinking she was asleep[4].

Sue arranged[5] her board and began a pen-and-ink[6] drawing to illustrate[7] a magazine story. Young artists must find their ways to true Art by drawing pictures for magazine stories that young authors[8] must write to find their ways to true Literature[9].

As Sue was sketching a pair of elegant[10] trousers and a cowboy hat on the figure[11] of the hero, an Idaho cowboy, she heard a low sound, several times repeated. She went quickly to the bedside.

1. scarcely [`skersli] (adv.) 幾乎不
2. make a move 移動
3. bedsheet [`bedʃi:t] (n.) 床單
4. asleep [ə`sli:p] (a.) 睡著的
5. arrange [ə`reɪndʒ] (v.) 安排；準備
6. pen-and-ink 鋼筆畫
7. illustrate [`ɪləstreɪt] (v.) 描繪；畫草圖
8. author [`ɔ:θər] (n.) 作者
9. literature [`lɪtərɪtʃər] (n.) 文學
10. elegant [`elɪɡənt] (a.) 優雅好看的
11. figure [`fɪɡjər] (n.) 人物
12. backward [`bækwərd] (adv.) 向後地

Johnsy's eyes were open wide. She was looking out the window and counting — counting backward[12].

"Twelve," she said, and a little later, "eleven"; and then "ten," and "nine"; and then "eight" and "seven," almost together.

✓ Check Up

The low sound Sue heard was that of Johnsy's _____ something.

Ans: counting

🎧 5

Sue looked curiously[1] out the window. What was there to count? There was only a bare[2], dreary[3] yard[4] to be seen, and the blank[5] side of the brick building eight meters away. An old, old ivy vine[6] climbed[7] halfway[8] up the brick wall. The cold breath[9] of autumn[10] had blown[11] its leaves[12] from the branches[13].

1. curiously [`kjʊriəsli] (adv.)
   好奇地
2. bare [ber] (a.) 光禿的
3. dreary [`drɪri] (a.)
   沉悶枯燥的
4. yard [jɑːrd] (n.) 後院
5. blank [blæŋk] (a.) 空白的
6. ivy vine 長春藤
7. climb [klaɪm] (v.) 攀爬
8. halfway [ˌhæf`weɪ] (adv.)
   一半地
9. breath [breθ] (n.) 呼吸

"What is it, dear?" asked Sue.

"Six," said Johnsy, in almost a whisper[14]. "They're falling[15] faster now. Three days ago, there were almost a hundred. It made my headache[16] to count them. But now it's easy. There goes another one. There are only five left now."

"Five what, dear? Tell your Susie."

"Leaves. On the ivy vine. When the last one falls, I must go, too. I've known that for three days. Didn't the doctor tell you?"

10. autumn [ˋɔːtəm] (n.) 秋天
11. blow [bloʊ] (v.) 吹
12. leaf [liːf] (n.) 樹葉
13. branch [bræntʃ] (n.) 分枝

14. in a whisper 低語著
15. fall [fɔːl] (v.) 掉落
16. headache [ˋhedeɪk] (v.) 頭痛

Check Up

Johnsy was counting the leaves because _____.

ⓐ she was too bored and sleepy
ⓑ she needed to do something not to sleep
ⓒ she identified the leaves with herself

Ans: c

25

"Oh, I've never heard of such nonsense," complained[1] Sue, with magnificent[2] scorn[3].

"What do old ivy leaves have to do with[4] your getting well? And you used to love that vine, you silly[5] girl. Why, the doctor told me this morning that your chances for getting well very soon were — let's see exactly[6] what he said — he said the chances were ten to one! Why, that's almost as good a chance as we have in New York when we ride on[7] the subway[8] or walk past a new building. Try to eat some soup now and let Susie go back to her drawing, so she can sell it to the editor[9]. Then I'll buy some port wine[10] for my sick friend, and pork chops[11] for my own greedy[12] self[13]."

---

1. complain [kəm`pleɪn] (v.)
   抱怨
2. magnificent [mæg`nɪfɪsənt] (a.) 極度的
3. scorn [skɔːrn] (n.) 嘲諷
4. have to do with...
   與……有關
5. silly [`sɪli] (a.) 傻氣的
6. exactly [ɪg`zæktli] (adv.)
   確切地

"You don't have to get any more wine," said Johnsy, keeping her eyes fixed[14] out the window. "There goes another. No, I don't want any broth[15]. That leaves just four. I want to see the last one fall before it gets dark. Then I'll go, too."

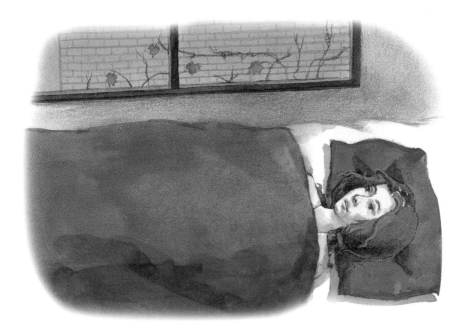

7. ride on 搭乘
8. subway [`sʌbweɪ] (n.) 地下鐵
9. editor [`edɪtər] (n.) 編輯
10. port wine 波特葡萄酒
11. pork chop 豬排
12. greedy [`griːdi] (a.) 貪心的
13. self [self] (n.) 自我
14. fix [fɪks] (v.) 固定
15. broth [brɑːθ] (n.) 湯品

"Johnsy, dear," said Sue, bending over[1] her, "will you promise me to keep your eyes closed and not to look out the window until I am done working? I must hand[2] those drawings in by tomorrow. I need the light[3], or I would draw[4] the shade[5] down."

"Couldn't you draw in the other room?" asked Johnsy, coldly.

"I'd rather[6] be here by you," said Sue. "Besides[7], I don't want you to keep looking at those silly ivy leaves."

"Tell me as soon as you have finished," said Johnsy, closing her eyes and lying white and still[8] as a fallen statue[9], "because I want to see the last one fall. I'm tired of[10] waiting. I'm tired of thinking. I want to let go of[11] everything and go sailing[12] down, down, just like one of those poor, tired leaves."

1. bend over 趴
   (bend-bent-bent)
2. hand in 繳交
3. light [laɪt] (n.) 光線
4. draw down 畫下
   (draw-drew-drawn)
5. shade [ʃeɪd] (n.) 陰影
6. would rather
   寧願……而不……
7. besides [bɪ`saɪdz] (adv.)
   而且；此外

"Try to sleep," said Sue. "I must call Behrman up[13] to be my model for the old Western miner[14]. I'll be right back. Don't move until I come back."

8. still [stɪl] (a.) 靜止不動
9. statue [`stætʃuː] (n.) 雕像
10. be tired of 對…感到厭倦
11. let go of 對……放手
12. go sailing 啟航
   (在書中有離開之意)
13. call up 呼喚
14. miner [`maɪnər] (n.) 礦工

A True or False.

T F **1** Greenwich Village was perfect for artists who wanted to escape from bill collectors.

T F **2** Johnsy was from the cold north; Sue was from the warm south.

T F **3** Johnsy and Sue met in college as roommates.

T F **4** Sue made money by drawing advertisements for magazines.

B Fill in the blanks with the given words.

whistle	sketch	get well	count	look

1 As Sue was _____ a cowboy, she heard a low moaning sound.

2 Johnsy lay on her bed _____ through her window at a brick wall.

3 What do old ivy leaves have to do with your _____?

4 Sue came into Johnsy's room, _____ a popular tune.

5 Johnsy was _____ backward: "Eight-seven-six . . . "

C Choose the correct answer.

1 What does Johnsy believe?

(a) She believes she will die when the night falls.

(b) She believes she will die when the first snowflake falls.

(c) She believes she will die when the last leaf falls from the ivy.

2 What does the doctor tell Sue?

(a) That Johnsy's chances of survival will increase if she becomes interested in fashion.

(b) That Johnsy must find the will to live.

(c) That Johnsy should move to a warmer apartment.

D Fill in the blanks with the given words.

> unseen   climbed   breath   touching   blown

- In November, a cold, **1** _____ stranger whom the doctors called pneumonia came to Greenwich Village, **2** _____ people here and there with his icy fingers.

- An old, old ivy vine **3** _____ halfway up the brick wall. The cold **4** _____ of autumn had **5** _____ its leaves from the branches.

Chapter Two

The Masterpiece

Old Behrman was a German painter who lived on the ground floor[1] beneath[2] them. He was past sixty and had a beard like Michelangelo's Moses curling[3] down from his wide head. Behrman was a failure[4] in art. He had been painting for forty years, but he had never produced anything noteworthy[5]. He had always been ready to paint a masterpiece[6], but he never actually started one. For several years, he had painted nothing except a small graphic now and then for an advertisement[7].

---

1. ground floor 底層樓（即一樓）
2. beneath [bɪ`ni:θ] (adv.)
   在……之下
3. curl [kɜːrl] (v.) 捲曲
4. failure [`feɪljər] (n.) 失敗
5. noteworthy [`noutˌwɜːrði] (a.)
   顯著的；值得注意的
6. masterpiece [`mæstərpi:s]
   (n.) 曠世巨作；傑作
7. advertisement
   [ˌædvər`taɪzmənt] (n.) 廣告
8. earn [ɜːrn] (v.) 賺得
9. colony [`kɑːləni] (n.)
   殖民地（文中指聚集處）

He earned[8] a little money by serving as a model to young artists in the colony[9] who could not afford a professional model. He drank a lot of gin[10] and still talked about the masterpiece he would paint one day. He was a fierce[11] little old man, who severely[12] criticized[13] softness[14] in anyone. He regarded himself as a bulldog ready to protect[15] the two young artists in the studio above.

10. gin [dʒɪn] (n.)
    琴酒；酒類（俚語）
11. fierce [fɪrs] (a.)
    激進的；凶惡的
12. severely [sɪ`vɪrəli] (adv.)
    嚴厲地
13. criticize [`krɪtɪsaɪz] (v.)
    挑剔；批評
14. softness [`sɑːftnɪs] (n.)
    軟弱；溫和
15. protect [prə`tekt] (v.) 保護

9

Sue found Behrman smelling strongly of wine in his dimly[1] lit[2] den[3] below. In one corner was a blank canvas on an easel[4] that had been waiting for twenty-five years to receive the first line[5] of a masterpiece.

She told him of Johnsy's idea. She explained how she feared[6] that Johnsy would indeed[7] float[8] away herself like a leaf when she became too weak. Old Behrman's eyes were dripping with[9] tears, but he shouted his contempt[10] for such idiotic[11] thoughts[12].

"What!" he cried. "Are there people in the world with the foolishness[13] to die because leaves drop off[14] from a simple vine? I have never heard of such a thing. No, I will not pose[15] as a model for you. Why do you allow such silly thoughts to come into Johnsy's brain[16]? Oh, the poor little Miss Johnsy."

1. dimly [`dɪmli] (adv.) 昏暗不明地
2. light [laɪt] (v.) 照亮
3. den [den] (n.) 小窩
4. easel [`izəl] (n.) 畫板
5. line [laɪn] (n.) 一劃
6. fear [fɪr] (v.) 害怕；恐懼

"She is very ill and weak," said Sue, "and the fever[17] has left her mind gloomy[18] and full of strange ideas. Very well, Mr. Behrman, if you do not care to[19] pose for me, you don't have to. But I think you are a terrible old man."

7. indeed [ɪn`diːd] (adv.) 真正地
8. float [floʊt] (v.) 漂流
9. drip with 充溢滿
10. contempt [kən`tempt] (n.) 藐視；輕視
11. idiotic [ɪdi`ɑːtik] (a.) 愚蠢的
12. thought [θɔːt] (n.) 想法
13. foolishness [`fuːlɪʃnɪs] (n.) 愚昧
14. drop off 落下
15. pose [poʊz] (v.) 擺姿勢
16. brain [breɪn] (n.) 大腦
17. fever [`fiːvər] (n.) 發燒
18. gloomy [`gluːmi] (a.) 憂鬱的
19. care to 願意；喜愛

"You are just like a woman!" yelled Behrman. "Who said I will not pose? Go on. I come with you. For half an hour, I have been trying to say that I am ready to pose. God! This is not a place in which one so good as Miss Johnsy should lie sick. Someday I will paint a masterpiece, and we shall all go away[1]. God, yes."

Johnsy was sleeping when they went upstairs. Sue pulled the shade down to the window sill[2] and motioned to[3] Behrman to come into the other room. From there, they looked out the window fearfully[4] at the ivy vine. Then they looked at each other for a moment[5] without[6] speaking. A persistent[7], cold rain was falling, mingled with[8] snow. Behrman, in his old blue shirt, took his seat[9] as the Western miner.

1. go away 離開
2. window sill 窗臺
3. motion to 示意去……
4. fearfully [`fɪrfəli] (adv.) 懼怕地
5. for a moment 一陣子
6. without [wɪð`aʊt] (prep.) 沒有……
7. persistent [pər`sɪstənt] (a.) 持續的
8. mingled with 與……混合
9. take one's seat 坐下
10. awake [ə`weɪk] (a.) 醒著的
11. dull [dʌl] (a.) 呆滯的
12. stare at 睜大眼睛看；瞪

When Sue awoke[10] from an hour's sleep the next morning, she found Johnsy with dull[11], wide-open eyes staring at[12] the drawn green shade.

"Pull it up[1]. I want to see," Johnsy ordered[2], in a whisper.

Wearily[3] Sue obeyed[4]. But, wait! After the beating[5] rain and fierce gusts[6] of wind that blew through the entire night, there yet remained against the brick wall one ivy leaf.

It was the last on the vine. Still dark green near its stem[7], but with its serrated[8] edges[9] tinted with[10] the yellow of dissolution[11] and decay[12], it hung[13] bravely[14] from a branch some twenty feet above the ground.

1. pull up 拉起
2. order [ˋɔːrdər] (v.) 命令
3. wearily [ˋwɪrəli] (adv.) 疲倦地；厭煩地
4. obey [ouˋbeɪ] (v.) 服從
5. beat [biːt] (v.) 打擊
6. gust [gʌst] (n.) 狂風
7. stem [stem] (n.) 莖；葉柄
8. serrated [ˋsereɪtɪd] (a.) 鋸齒狀的
9. edge [edʒ] (n.) 邊緣
10. tinted with 被……所著色
11. dissolution [dɪsəˋluːʃən] (n.) 終止；消失
12. decay [dɪˋkeɪ] (n.) 衰敗
13. hang [hæŋ] (v.) 懸掛
14. bravely [ˋbreɪvli] (adv.) 勇敢無懼地
15. at the same time 同一時間

"It is the last one," said Johnsy. "I thought it would surely fall during the night. I heard the wind. It will fall today, and I shall die at the same time[15]."

"Dear, dear!" said Sue, leaning[16] her worn[17] face down to the pillow[18], "Think of me if you won't think of yourself. What would I do?"

But Johnsy did not answer. The loneliest[19] thing in all the world is a soul[20] when it is making ready to go on its final mysterious[21], far journey. The idea seemed to possess[22] her more strongly as one by one, the ties[23] that bound[24] her to friendship and to earth were loosened[25].

16. lean [liːn] (v.) 斜靠著；倚著
17. worn [wɔːrn] (a.)
     憔悴的；精疲力竭的
18. pillow [`pɪloʊ] (n.) 枕頭
19. lonely [`loʊnli] (a.)
     寂寞的；孤獨的
20. soul [soʊl] (n.) 靈魂；心靈

21. mysterious [mɪ`stɪriəs] (a.)
     神秘不可知的
22. possess [pə`zes] (v.)
     擁有；控制支配
23. tie [taɪ] (n.) 聯繫；連結
24. bind [baɪnd] (v.) 綁；束縛
25. loosen [`luːsən] (v.)
     鬆開；放鬆

The day wore away[1], and even through the twilight[2] they could still see the lone[3] ivy leaf clinging to[4] its stem against the wall. And then, with the coming of the night, the north wind again howled[5], while the rain still beat against the windows and dripped down[6] from the low eaves[7].

1. **wear away** 磨掉；減少
2. **twilight** [ˈtwaɪlaɪt] (n.) 黃昏；朦朧
3. **lone** [loun] (a.) 孤單寂寞的
4. **cling to** 依附著
5. **howl** [haʊl] (v.) 呼嘯
6. **drip down** 滴落
7. **eaves** [iːvz] (n.) 屋簷
8. **mercilessly** [ˈmɜːrsəlɪsli] (adv.) 毫不留情地

When it was light enough, Johnsy mercilessly[8] commanded[9] that the shade be raised[10].

The ivy leaf was still there. Johnsy lay for a long time looking at it. And then she called to Sue, who was stirring[11] her chicken soup over the gas stove.

"I've been a bad girl, Susie," said Johnsy. "Something has made that last leaf stay there to show me how bad I was. It is a sin[12] to want to die. You may bring me a little soup now, and some milk with a little wine in it. Wait, pack[13] some pillows about me, and I will sit up and watch you cook."

An hour later, she said, "Susie, some day I hope to paint the Bay of Naples."

The last leaf gave Johnsy _____.

a sorrow and despair
b hope to succeed
c the will to live

Ans: c

9. command [kə`mænd] (v.)
命令；指揮
10. raise [reɪz] (v.) 升高；抬起

11. stir [stɜːr] (v.) 攪動
12. sin [sɪn] (n.) 罪惡；過錯
13. pack [pæk] (v.) 堆積

The doctor came in the afternoon, and Sue went into the hallway with him as he left.

"Even[1] chances," said the doctor, taking Sue's thin, shaking[2] hand in his. "With good nursing[3], you'll win. And now I must see another case I have downstairs. Behrman, his name is — some kind of an artist, I believe. Pneumonia, too. He is an old, weak man, and the attack[4] is severe. There is no hope for him, but he goes to the hospital today to be made more comfortable[5]."

The next day, the doctor said to Sue, "She's out of danger[6]. You've won[7]. Nutrition[8] and care[9] now — that's all."

And that afternoon, Sue came to the bed where Johnsy lay, happily knitting[10] a very blue and very useless[11] woolen[12] scarf. Sue put one arm around Johnsy, pillows, and all.

1. even [ˋiːvən] (a.) 均等的
2. shaking [ˋʃeɪkɪŋ] (a.) 顫抖的
3. nursing [ˋnɜːrsɪŋ] (n.) 照顧
4. attack [əˋtæk] (n.) 攻擊
5. comfortable [ˋkʌmfərtəbəl] (a.) 舒適的
6. out of danger 脫離險境
7. win [wɪn] (v.) 勝利
8. nutrition [nuːˋtrɪʃən] (n.) 營養
9. care [ker] (n.) 細心照料
10. knit [nɪt] (v.) 織
11. useless [ˋjuːsləs] (a.) 無用的
12. woolen [ˋwʊlən] (a.) 羊毛的

✔ Check Up

True or False.

ⓐ The doctor asked Sue to look after Behrman. _____
ⓑ Behrman got pneumonia because of a lack of nutrition. _____

Ans: ⓐ F ⓑ F

43

14

"I have something to tell you, white mouse," she said. "Mr. Behrman died of[1] pneumonia today in the hospital. He was ill only two days. The janitor[2] found him on the morning of the first day in his room downstairs helpless with[3] pain[4]. His shoes and clothing were completely[5] wet and icy cold. They couldn't imagine[6] where he had been on such a dreadful[7] night."

"And then they found a lantern[8], still lit, and a ladder[9] that had been dragged[10] from its place, and some scattered[11] brushes[12], and a palette with green and yellow colors mixed[13] on it, and — look out the window, dear, at the last ivy leaf on the wall. Didn't you wonder why it never fluttered[14] or moved when the wind blew? Ah, darling, it's Behrman's masterpiece — he painted it there the night that the last leaf fell."

1. **die of** 死於
2. **janitor** [`dʒænətər] (n.) 工友；樓管
3. **helpless with** 無助於……
4. **pain** [peɪn] (n.) 痛苦
5. **completely** [kəm`pliːtli] (adv.) 完全地
6. **imagine** [ɪ`mædʒɪn] (v.) 想像
7. **dreadful** [`dredfəl] (a.) 糟糕的
8. **lantern** [`læntərn] (n.) 提燈
9. **ladder** [`lædər] (n.) 梯子
10. **drag** [dræg] (v.) 拖拉
11. **scatter** [`skætər] (v.) 散佈
12. **brush** [brʌʃ] (n.) 刷子；筆刷
13. **mix** [mɪks] (v.) 混合
14. **flutter** [`flʌtər] (v.) 顫動

✓ Check Up

The last leaf did not move because it was _____ on the wall.

ⓐ pasted　　　ⓑ painted　　　ⓒ put

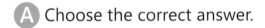

Comprehension Quiz　Chapter Two

A Choose the correct answer.

1 What was old Behrman's masterpiece?

(a) He never painted a masterpiece.

(b) He painted a leaf on the wall of the building.

(c) He painted a very realistic painting of an old miner.

2 How did Behrman die?

(a) He died of old age.

(b) He drank too much wine and fell down.

(c) He got very cold and wet when he painted outside.

B Match.

1 Johnsy　　　•

2 Sue　　　•

3 The doctor　•

4 Behrman　•

• **A** spoke in terms of probability.

• **B** showed contempt for people who were weak.

• **C** knitted a very blue and very useless scarf.

• **D** stirred chicken soup on the stove.

C True or False.

T F **1** Behrman was very protective of Sue and Johnsy.

T F **2** The doctor did not put all his faith in medicine alone.

T F **3** Behrman would not pose for Sue.

T F **4** After Raoul left Christine's room, he heard her say, "I only sing for you, Raoul."

T F **5** Two leaves remained on the ivy branch for many days.

D Match the two parts of each sentence.

1 The last leaf hung bravely from the branch   •   • **A** and I will watch you cook.

2 Even after the strong gusts of wind,   •   • **B** on such a cold and windy night.

3 They couldn't imagine where he had been   •   • **C** and dripped down from the eaves.

4 Pack some pillows around me,   •   • **D** against the brick wall.

5 The rain still beat against the windows   •   • **E** one leaf remained on the branch.

Unexpected Humanity

Although O. Henry certainly did not invent[1] the short story, he mastered[2] this form and perfected[3] the technique of the surprise ending.

O. Henry became a master at doing this by laying the construction[4] for these endings in the story itself. He gives hints to his readers of the endings to come by briefly including details that seem unimportant at first mention[5], but become immensely[6] important when the surprise ending is "revealed[7]". An example of this is in the story "The Last Leaf" where the reader sees clues[8] of what the old artist living downstairs has done to save the life of the girl upstairs.

---

1. invent [ɪn`vɛnt] (v.) 發明
2. master [`mæstər] (v.) 精通於
3. perfect [`pɜːrfɪkt] (v.) 使完美
4. construction [kən`strʌkʃən] (n.) 架構
5. mention [`mɛnʃən] (n.) 提及
6. immensely [ɪ`mɛnsli] (adv.) 非常地
7. reveal [rɪ`viːl] (v.) 透露
8. clue [kluː] (n.) 線索

We know the old man has been waiting his whole life to paint his masterpiece, but we don't expect him to. Not until the very ending do we realize that the old artist has indeed fulfilled[9] his dream while at the  same time, fatally[10] injuring[11] himself in a selfless[12] act of kindness.

O. Henry is a master at leading the reader down one path of expectation, and then shattering[13] these expectations at the surprising conclusion[14] of the story. However, just as in "The Last Leaf", these endings are rarely random[15] acts of cruel fate. Instead, they are carefully constructed[16] by the masterful author to show the reader the humanity of our frail[17] and sometimes foolish, but also generous[18] and kind nature[19].

---

9. fulfill [fʊl`fɪl] (v.) 完成
10. fatally [`feɪtəli] (adv.) 致命地
11. injure [`ɪndʒər] (v.) 傷害
12. selfless [`selflɪs] (a.) 無私的
13. shatter [`ʃætər] (v.) 粉碎
14. conclusion [kən`klu:ʒən] (n.) 結果
15. random [`rændəm] (a.) 隨機的
16. construct [kən`strʌkt] (v.) 建構
17. frail [freɪl] (a.) 意志薄弱的
18. generous [`dʒenərəs] (a.) 慷慨大方的
19. nature [`neɪtʃər] (n.) 本性

The Cop and the Anthem

警察與讚美詩

Chapter One

15

Soapy's Winter Plans

Soapy moved uneasily[1] on his bench in Madison Square, New York City. Wild geese[2] were honking[3] overhead[4] on their way south. Wives without fur coats[5] suddenly became kinder to their husbands as they strolled[6] on the streets in front of the shops. When you see these things, you know that winter is coming.

A dead leaf fell into Soapy's lap[7]. That leaf was Jack Frost's[8] calling card[9]. Jack is kind enough to the inhabitants[10] of Madison Square to warn[11] them that he is coming soon. At every corner, he hands[12] these cards to the North Wind, so that all who receive one can

1. uneasily [ʌn`i:zəli] (adv.) 踢促不安地
2. goose [gu:s] (n.) 鵝；雁
3. honk [hɑŋk] (v.) 鳴叫
4. overhead [`ouvərhed] (adv.) 高高地
5. fur coat 毛皮大衣
6. stroll [stroul] (v.) 閒逛
7. lap [læp] (n.) 膝上部
8. Jack Frost 冬日之神
9. calling card 名片

make plans [13] for the coming freezing [14]
weather.

Soapy knew that he had to start thinking of
ways to deal with [15] the difficulties [16] of colder
weather.

How would he stay warm? Where would he
sleep? This is why he moved uneasily on his
park bench.

10. inhabitant [ɪn`hæbɪtənt] (n.)
　　居民
11. warn [wɔ:rn] (v.) 警告
12. hand [hænd] (v.) 傳遞
13. make a plan 計畫

14. freezing [`fri:zɪŋ] (a.)
　　冰冷的
15. deal with 處理；面對
16. difficulty [`dɪfɪkəlti] (n.)
　　困難

Soapy did not have great ambitions[1] for his annual[2] winter hibernation[3]. He did not dream about cruising[4] on a ship in the Mediterranean[5]. Instead, he just wanted three months on Blackwell's Island. There he would surely have three hot meals a day and a warm bed every night. Also, he would have good company[6] with whom to spend the winter days. This was as high as Soapy dared to[7] dream.

1. ambition [æmˋbɪʃən] (n.)
   野心；抱負
2. annual [ˋænjuəl] (a.)
   年度的
3. hibernation [haɪbərˋneɪʃən]
   (n.) 過冬；冬眠
4. cruise [kruːz] (v.)
   航行；漫遊
5. the Mediterranean (n.)
   地中海
6. company [ˋkʌmpəni] (n.)
   夥伴；陪伴
7. dare to 敢⋯⋯

For the past several winters, the prison[8] on Blackwell's Island had been Soapy's home. While his more fortunate[9] neighbors made their winter plans to vacation in sunny southern spots[10], Soapy made plans to move into Blackwell Prison.

And now the time had come. The previous[11] night was so cold that even after stuffing[12] three Sunday newspapers under his clothes, Soapy had still been cold. He could not sleep on his bench near the spurting[13] fountain[14] in the ancient[15] square.

8. prison [`prɪzən] (n.) 監獄
9. fortunate [`fɔːrtʃənət] (a.)
   幸運的
10. spot [spɑːt] (n.)
    旅遊聖地；地點
11. previous [`priːvɪəs] (a.)
    之前的

12. stuff [stʌf] (v.) 塞；填充
13. spurt [spɜːrt] (v.) 噴射
14. fountain [`faʊntən] (n.)
    噴泉
15. ancient [`eɪnʃənt] (v.)
    古老的

 Check Up

True or False.

ⓐ Soapy badly needed a shelter for the winter. _____
ⓑ Soapy had not been in prison before. _____

17

Today, Soapy could think of nothing else but[1] the Island. He did not consider[2] asking for[3] charity[4]. In Soapy's mind, the legal[5] system was kinder than charitable institutions[6]. There were many such institutions, both civil[7] and religious[8], that would give help to Soapy if he asked. However, to Soapy's proud[9] way of thinking, charity came with a price. His pride[10] was hurt every time someone gave him something for free[11]. In addition[12], if he was given a bed, he would be required to[13] take a bath[14].

If he accepted bread, the person giving it would often ask many very personal questions.

1. but [bʌt] (prep.)
   除了……以外
2. consider [kən`sɪdər] (v.)
   考慮
3. ask for 要求
4. charity [`tʃærəti] (n.)
   慈悲；善舉
5. legal [`liːgəl] (a.) 法律的
6. charitable institution
   慈善機構
7. civil [`sɪvəl] (a.)
   公民的；民間的
8. religious [rɪ`lɪdʒəs] (a.)
   宗教的
9. proud [praʊd] (a.)
   自尊的；有志氣的
10. pride [praɪd] (n.) 驕傲
11. for free 免費
12. in addition 另外
13. be required to
    被要求做……
14. take a bath 洗澡
15. follow [`fɑːloʊ] (v.)
    追隨；遵循
16. rule [ruːl] (n.) 規則
17. involve A with B
    使 A 涉及 B
18. personal affairs 個人事務

"No way," thought Soapy about going to a charitable institution. "It's much better to be a guest of the law. The law always follows[15] the same rules[16], and it does not involve[17] itself with one's personal affairs[18]."

 Check Up

Soapy did not want charity because charitable people _____.

a asked him bothering questions
b forced him to go to church
c wanted him to get a public education

Ans: a

18

Soapy was determined to[1] go to the Island, but he had to decide how to get there. There were many easy ways of doing this. The most pleasant one was to eat a fabulous[2] meal at an expensive restaurant and then announce[3] he could not pay. He would go quietly with the police when they were called. Then a judge[4] would give him a ticket[5] to the Island for at least the entire winter.

Having set his mind on[6] this objective[7], Soapy got up off his bench and walked out of the square. He crossed[8] the intersection of Broadway and Fifth Avenue and turned up Broadway. He stopped in front of a glittering[9] cafe where many delicious items[10] were displayed[11].

1. be determined to
   下定決心……
2. fabulous [ˋfæbjʊləs] (a.)
   極好的
3. announce [əˋnaʊns] (v.)
   聲稱;宣布
4. judge [dʒʌdʒ] (n.) 法官
5. ticket 傳票
6. set one's mind on
   決定好要……
7. objective [əbˋdʒɛktɪv] (n.)
   目標

8. cross [krɑːs] (v.) 穿越
9. glittering [ˋglɪtərɪŋ] (a.)
   發亮的
10. item [ˋaɪtəm] (n.) 品項
11. display [dɪˋspleɪ] (v.) 展示
12. appearance [əˋpɪrəns] (n.)
    外觀
13. vest [vɛst] (n.) 背心
14. clean-shaven
    (鬍子)刮得乾淨的
15. missionary [ˋmɪʃəneri] (a.)
    傳教的;教會的

Soapy had confidence in his appearance[12] from the lowest button of his vest[13] upward. His face was clean-shaven[14], and his coat was nice. He was wearing a new tie that had been given to him by a lady missionary[15] on Thanksgiving Day, just a few weeks ago.

If he could make it to[1] a table in the restaurant and sit down, Soapy would succeed in[2] his plan. His lower body would not be visible[3] to the waiter as he ordered the most expensive meal on the menu, along with[4] a bottle of fine wine and an expensive cigar.

"I'll have a roasted[5] duck," thought Soapy. He figured[6] that he would not run up[7] a huge bill so that the restaurant owner[8] would demand[9] revenge[10]. However, the meal would be enough to make him happy at the start of his voyage[11] to his winter home.

1. make it to 順利去……
2. succeed in 成功
3. visible [`vɪzɪbl̩] (a.) 看得見的
4. along with 伴隨著……
5. roasted [`roustɪd] (a.) 火烤的
6. figure [`fɪgjər] (v.) 以為
7. run up 積欠
8. owner [`ounər] (n.) 所有者
9. demand [dɪ`mænd] (v.) 要求
10. revenge [rɪ`vendʒ] (n.) 報復
11. voyage [`vɔɪɪdʒ] (n.) 旅行
12. set foot 邁開步伐
13. suspiciously [sə`spɪʃəsli] (adv.) 存有懷疑地

With these happy thoughts, Soapy entered
the cafe. However, as soon as he set foot[12]
inside the door, the head waiter looked at him
suspiciously[13]. The waiter saw Soapy's old
and frayed[14] trousers, as well as[15] his ruined[16]
shoes. Suddenly, Soapy felt the strong hands
of several waiters on his shoulders and back
as he was quietly and quickly turned around
and pushed back outside.

Soapy left Broadway.

It seemed that his
route[17] to the Island of
his desire[18] would not
involve food. He had
to think of another
way to get to his
winter haven[19].

14. frayed [`freɪd] (a.) 磨損的
15. as well as 和……
16. ruined [`ruːɪnd] (a.) 毀壞的
17. route [ruːt] (n.) 路線；路程
18. desire [dɪ`zaɪr] (n.) 渴望
19. haven [`heɪvən] (n.) 避風港；躲避處所

🎧 20

At a corner of Sixth Avenue, a large glass window attracted Soapy's attention. It was a beautiful sight[1], with Christmas lights and a nice display showing off[2] the store's products. Soapy picked up a stone and threw it through the glass.

1. sight [saɪt] (n.) 景象
2. show off 展示出
3. in the lead 領頭
4. stand still 不動地站著
5. at the sight of 看到⋯⋯
6. badge [bædʒ] (n.) 徽章
7. officer [`ɑːfɪsər] (n.) 警察
8. have something to do with 與⋯⋯有關
9. refuse to 拒絕
10. suspect [sə`spekt] (n.) 嫌疑犯
11. smash [smæʃ] (v.) 砸碎
12. stick around 逗留於⋯⋯

The Cop and the Anthem

People came running around the corner, a policeman in the lead[3]. Soapy stood still[4], with his hands in his pockets, and smiled at the sight of[5] the policeman's badge[6].

"Where's the man who did that?" asked the officer[7] excitedly.

"Don't you think that I might have had something to do with[8] it?" said Soapy in a friendly voice, as he welcomed his good fortune.

The policeman's mind refused to[9] accept Soapy as a suspect[10]. Men who smash[11] windows do not stick around[12] to talk to policemen. Men like that run away. The policeman saw a man halfway down the block running to catch a car. He took out[13] his club[14] and ran after the unfortunate citizen[15]. Soapy, with disgust[16] in his heart, went away, twice unsuccessful[17].

 Check Up

How did Soapy probably feel when he wasn't arrested?
[a] Disappointed   [b] Relieved   [c] Ashamed

Ans: a

13. take out 拿出
14. club [klʌb] (n.) 棍子
15. citizen [`sɪtɪzən] (n.) 市民
16. with disgust 帶有厭惡地
17. unsuccessful [ˌʌnsək`sesfəl] (a.) 不成功的

On the opposite[1] side of the street was an average-looking restaurant. Its regular customers[2] were people with large appetites[3] who could not pay a lot for a meal. The plates and atmosphere[4] were thick[5]; its soup and tablecloths[6] thin. Soapy walked inside with his old shoes and ragged[7] pants, and no one challenged[8] him. He sat at a table and ate a large steak, pancakes, doughnuts, and a piece of pie. At the end of his meal, he confessed[9] to the waiter that he had not even a penny in his pockets.

"Now, get busy and call a cop[10]," said Soapy. "And don't keep a gentleman waiting."

1. opposite [ˋɑːpəzɪt] (a.) 相反的；對面的
2. regular customer 常客
3. appetite [ˋæpɪtaɪt] (n.) 胃口
4. atmosphere [ˋætməsfɪr] (n.) 氣氛
5. thick [θɪk] (a.) 厚的
6. tablecloth [ˋteɪbəlklɑːθ] (n.) 桌布
7. ragged [ˋrægɪd] (a.) 破舊的
8. challenge [ˋtʃælɪndʒ] (v.) 指責；有異議

The Cop and the Anthem

"No cop for you," said the waiter. He had a thick voice and red eyes. He called another waiter, who was larger and stronger. "Hey, Con!"

The two waiters threw Soapy out onto the hard street. He landed[11] on his left ear. Soapy got up slowly, limb by limb[12], checking for[13] broken bones[14]. Satisfied that he was not seriously injured[15], he beat the dust[16] from his clothes.

Arrest[17] seemed like but a faraway dream. The Island seemed a distant paradise.

A policeman who stood before a drugstore two doors away laughed and walked down the street.

9. confess [kənˋfes] (v.) 坦白
10. cop [kɑːp] (n.) 警察 (俗稱)
11. land [lænd] (v.) 著地
12. limb [lɪm] (n.) 肢臂
13. check for 察看
14. bone [boʊn] (n.) 骨頭
15. injure [ˋɪndʒər] (v.) 受傷
16. dust [dʌst] (n.) 灰塵
17. arrest [əˋrest] (n.) 逮捕

A Fill in the blanks with the given words.

quietly   suspiciously   excitedly   uneasily

❶ Soapy moved _____ on his park bench because winter was coming.

❷ The cop _____ asked Soapy which way the man who broke the window went.

❸ The waiter looked at Soapy's frayed pants _____.

❹ _____, the waiters pushed Soapy outside before he could sit down.

B Match the two parts of each sentence.

❶ Soapy wanted to be arrested •

❷ The cop didn't suspect Soapy •

❸ Soapy didn't want to ask for charity •

❹ Soapy didn't want to run up a huge bill •

❺ Soapy broke a window •

• Ⓐ because he liked his privacy.

• Ⓑ so that he would have a warm home.

• Ⓒ in the hopes of being arrested.

• Ⓓ because he didn't run away.

• Ⓔ so that the owner would not seek revenge.

C True or False.

T F **1** Soapy was planning to escape the winter cold by moving south.

T F **2** Soapy usually spent the winter in Blackwell Prison.

T F **3** Soapy ate a nice roasted duck in the glittering cafe.

T F **4** The cop thought the man running after a car broke the window.

D Rearrange the following sentences in chronological order.

1 Soapy was cold at night even though he put newspapers under his clothes.

2 Soapy broke a large window.

3 Soapy entered a fancy cafe.

4 Soapy left his park bench in Madison Square.

5 Soapy decided to get arrested.

_____ ⇨ _____ ⇨ _____ ⇨ _____ ⇨ _____

Chapter Two

Soapy Is Doomed to[1] Failure

Soapy traveled five blocks before he gained[2] enough courage[3] to try again. This time, he found an opportunity[4] that he was sure would end in[5] success. A young, pretty woman was standing before a shop window looking at a display of coffee mugs[6] and silverware[7] with great interest.

1. be doomed to 注定要……
2. gain [geɪn] (v.) 得到
3. courage [`kɜːrɪdʒ] (n.) 勇氣
4. opportunity [ˌɑːpər`tuːnəti] (n.) 機會
5. end in 結束於
6. mug [mʌg] (n.) 馬克杯
7. silverware [`sɪlvərwer] (n.) 銀器

Just two meters away, a large policeman with a stern[8] expression leaned against the wall of the building.

Soapy's plan was to bother[9] the lady and be arrested for harassment[10]. The woman was obviously[11] from the respectable[12] middle class[13]; he would make himself look like a drunken bum[14]. The strict cop would surely arrest him, and soon he would be on his way to a warm cell[15] on the Island with a guaranteed[16] three meals a day.

Soapy straightened[17] his tie and arranged his pants so that they were easily seen as old and ragged. He set his face in an aggressive[18] expression and walked up to the young woman.

8. stern [stɜːrn] (a.)
   嚴格的；不動搖的
9. bother [ˋbɑːðər] (v.) 煩擾
10. harassment [ˋhærəsmənt]
    (n.) 騷擾
11. obviously [ˋɑːbviəsli] (adv.)
    明顯地
12. respectable [rɪˋspektəbl̩]
    (a.) 值得尊敬的
13. middle class 中產階級

14. bum [bʌm] (n.)
    流浪漢；吊兒郎當的人
15. cell [sel] (n.) 小囚房；巢室
16. guaranteed [ˌɡærənˋtiːd]
    (a.) 保證的
17. straighten [ˋstreɪtn̩] (v.)
    弄直；整頓
18. aggressive [əˋɡresɪv] (a.)
    具侵略性的

23

Soapy tried to make eye contact[1] and cleared his throat[2] loudly before speaking. He used different come-on[3] lines[4] with the woman, some of which were almost offensive[5] but not quite. Out of the corner of his eye, Soapy noticed that the policeman was looking at him steadily[6].

The young woman moved away a couple of steps and continued to look at the mugs on display. Soapy followed her, boldly[7] standing right next to her. He said, "Oh come on there, Julie. Don't you want to come and get a drink with me?"

The policeman was still looking. The harassed[8] young woman only had to raise a finger to call the policeman over, and then Soapy would be on his way to the Island.

1. make eye contact
   有眼神接觸
2. clear one's throat 清喉嚨
3. come-on 跟著來
   （此指搭訕用語）
4. line [laɪn] (n.) 臺詞
5. offensive [əˋfɛnsɪv] (a.)
   冒犯的
6. steadily [ˋstɛdəli] (adv.)
   沉著地
7. boldly [boʊldli] (adv.)
   大膽無恥地
8. harassed [ˋhærəst] (a.)
   被騷擾的
9. warmth [wɔːrmθ] (n.) 溫暖
10. police station 警察局
11. face [feɪs] (v.) 面對
12. sleeve [sliːv] (n.) 袖子
13. joyfully [ˋdʒɔɪfəli] (a.)
    開心喜悅地

Already, he could feel the warmth[9] of the police station[10].

Suddenly, the young woman faced[11] him and caught his coat sleeve[12] in her hand.

"Sure, Mike," she said joyfully[13], "if you'll buy me a few drinks. I would have spoken to you sooner, but the cop was watching."

24

With the young woman clinging to his arm as ivy clings to an oak tree[1], Soapy walked past the policeman. He was overcome with[2] gloom[3]. He seemed doomed to cold, lonely liberty[4].

At the next corner, he shook[5] the young woman's hand off his arm and ran. He halted[6] in a district where he knew people were more carefree[7] and lively at night. Women in furs and men in nice winter coats moved happily in the winter air.

A sudden fear overcame Soapy.

He wondered if some magic spell[8] had made him immune to arrest. This sudden thought made him panic[9] a little. At the same time, he came upon[10] another policeman who was standing in front of a brightly-lit theater. Soapy immediately had the idea of being arrested for "disorderly[11] conduct[12]".

1. oak tree (n.) 橡樹
2. be overcome with 為……所擊潰
3. gloom [glu:m] (n.) 沮喪
4. liberty [`lɪbərti] (n.) 自由
5. shake [ʃeɪk] (v.) 甩開
6. halt [hɑ:lt] (v.) 停頓
7. carefree [`kerfri:] (a.) 無憂無慮的
8. magic spell (n.) 魔咒
9. panic [`pænɪk] (v.) 害怕
10. come upon 遇見
11. disorderly [dɪs`ɔ:rdərli] (adv.) 失序地
12. conduct [kən`dʌkt] (n.) 行為
13. sidewalk [`sɪdwɔ:k] (n.) 人行道

On the sidewalk[13], Soapy began to yell drunken gibberish[14] at the top of his harsh[15] voice. He danced, howled[16], shouted crazily, and tried to disturb[17] passers-by[18] as best as he could.

14. gibberish [ˋdʒɪbərɪʃ] (n.) 胡言亂語
15. harsh [hɑːrʃ] (a.) 刺耳的
16. howl [haʊl] (v.) 大聲吼叫

17. disturb [dɪˋstɜːrb] (v.) 打擾
18. passer-by (n.) 路過的人

The policeman twirled[1] his club, turned his back to Soapy, and remarked[2] to a citizen, "It must be one of those Yale students celebrating their victory[3] over Hartford College in football. He is noisy, but no harm[4]. We have instructions[5] to leave them be[6]."

Now more gloomy than ever, Soapy stopped making noise. Would a policeman never arrest him? In his mind, the Island was an unattainable[7] paradise. He buttoned[8] his thin coat against the chill[9] wind and moved on down the street.

Through a liquor store[10] window, he saw a well-dressed[11] man buying a bottle of[12] wine. The man had put his silk umbrella by the door as he entered the store. Soapy stepped in[13] the door, took the umbrella, and walked slowly away. The well-dressed man came out of the store in a rush[14].

"My umbrella," he said sternly.

1. twirl [twɜːrl] (v.) 快速轉動
2. remark [rɪˋmɑːrk] (v.) 談論；說
3. victory [ˋvɪktəri] (n.) 勝利
4. harm [hɑːrm] (n.) 傷害
5. instruction [ɪnˋstrʌkʃən] (n.) 指揮；教導
6. leave A be B 讓 A 維持 B
7. unattainable [ˌʌnəˋteɪnəbəl] (a.) 無法達成的
8. button [ˋbʌtən] (v.) 扣上鈕扣
9. chill [tʃɪl] (a.) 寒冷的
10. liquor store (n.) 販酒商店
11. well-dressed (a.) 穿著體面的
12. a bottle of 一瓶
13. step in 踏入
14. in a rush 匆忙地

"Oh, is it?" sneered[1] Soapy, being as mean[2] as he could. "Well, why don't you call a policeman? I took it. Your umbrella! Why don't you call a cop? There's one on the corner."

The umbrella owner slowed down[3]. Soapy did likewise[4], thinking that luck would run against him again. The policeman looked at the two curiously.

"Of course," said the umbrella man, "that is . . . well, you know how these mistakes happen. I . . . if it's your umbrella, I hope you'll excuse[5] me. I picked it up[6] this morning in a restaurant. If you recognize[7] it as yours, why, I hope you'll. . . "

"Of course it's mine," said Soapy, viciously[8].

The ex-umbrella man retreated[9]. The policeman hurried[10] to assist[11] a tall blond woman in an opera cloak[12]. She was crossing the street in front of a truck that was approaching[13] just down the block.

1. sneer [snɪr] (v.) 諷刺嘲笑
2. mean [miːn] (a.) 卑鄙的
3. slow down 慢下來
4. likewise [ˈlaɪkwaɪz] (adv.) 也;一樣
5. excuse [ɪkˈskjuːz] (v.) 原諒
6. pick up 撿起
7. recognize [ˈrekəgnaɪz] (v.) 認出
8. viciously [ˈvɪʃəsli] (adv.) 邪惡地
9. retreat [rɪˈtriːt] (v.) 退避開;撤退
10. hurry [ˈhʌri] (v.) 急忙去
11. assist [əˈsɪst] (v.) 協助;幫忙
12. opera cloak (n.) 夜禮服斗篷
13. approach [əˈproutʃ] (v.) 接近

Soapy walked eastward[1] along a street that was under construction[2]. He threw the umbrella angrily into an open hole. He cursed[3] the men who wear helmets and carry clubs. Because he wanted to fall into their hands, they seemed to regard him as a king who could do no wrong[4].

Finally, Soapy reached one of the avenues to the east where it was much quieter. He walked down this street toward Madison Square. Even though his home was a park bench, he knew instinctively[5] where it was.

But on an unusually[6] quiet corner, Soapy came to a stop[7]. Here was an old church: old-fashioned[8] and cozy[9]. Through one violet-stained[10] window, a soft light glowed[11], where an organ player was making soft music.

He was probably practicing for next Sunday's mass[12]. Sweet music drifted[13] out to Soapy's ears. It caught and held him in an iron grip[14] outside the church gate[15].

1. eastward [ˋiːstwɔːrd] (adv.)
   向東地
2. under construction 施工中
3. curse [kɜːrs] (v.) 詛咒
4. do wrong 犯錯
5. instinctively [ɪnˋstɪŋktɪvli]
   (adv.) 發自本能地
6. unusually [ʌnˋjuːʒuəli]
   (adv.) 不尋常地
7. come to a stop 停止

8. old-fashioned (a.) 過時的
9. cozy [ˋkouzi] (a.) 愜意的
10. stained [steɪnd] (a.) 染色的
11. glow [ɡlou] (v.) 發光發亮
12. mass [mæs] (n.) 彌撒
13. drift [drɪft] (v.) 漂流
14. grip [ɡrɪp] (n.) 控制
15. gate [ɡeɪt] (n.)
    大門；圍牆門

1. vehicle [`vi:ɪkl] (n.) 車輛
2. pedestrian [pə`destriən] (n.) 行人
3. sparrow [`sperou] (n.) 麻雀
4. chirp [tʃɜːrp] (v.) 啾啾叫
5. for a little while 一小段時間裡
6. anthem [`ænθəm] (n.) 彌撒曲
7. motionless [`mouʃənləs] (a.) 靜止的

🎧 28

The moon was above, bright and calm; vehicles[1] and pedestrians[2] were few; sparrows[3] chirped[4] sleepily under the rooftops — for a little while[5], the scene might have been a country churchyard. And the anthem[6] that the organist played held Soapy motionless[7], for he had known it well in his younger days. Ah, the good old days when his life contained[8] loving parents, good friends, bright ambitions, and new, clean clothes.

The combination[9] of Soapy's tired but open mind and the feelings he experienced outside the church created a sudden and wonderful change in his heart.

To his sudden horror[10], he realized how terrible his life had become. His path[11] was a dead end, full of degradation[12], unworthy[13] desires, dead hopes, and dull senses[14]. He lived only to fulfill[15] his basic needs[16]. No grander[17] purposes like love, ambition, and the feeling of success even touched upon his lonely, miserable[18] life.

---

8. contain [kənˋteɪn] (v.) 包含
9. combination [ˌkɑːmbɪˋneɪʃən] (n.) 結合
10. to one's horror 令人恐懼的是
11. path [pæθ] (n.) 路途
12. degradation [ˌdegrəˋdeɪʃən] (n.) 墮落
13. unworthy [ʌnˋwɜːrðɪ] (a.) 不值得的
14. sense [sens] (n.) 理智
15. fulfill [fʊlˋfɪl] (v.) 滿足
16. needs [niːdz] (n.) 需求
17. grand [grænd] (a.) 偉大的
18. miserable [ˋmɪzərəbəl] (a.) 悲慘的

29

In a moment, his mind responded to[1] this new mood. A sudden and strong impulse[2] drove him to fight against his desperate[3] fate[4]. He would pull himself up out of his homeless condition[5]; he would make a man out of himself again. He would conquer[6] the evil[7] that had taken possession of him. There was time; he was still young. He would remember his old, eager[8] ambitions and pursue[9] them without failing.

Those solemn[10] but sweet organ notes[11] had caused a revolution[12] in his mind. Tomorrow, he would go into the busy downtown district and find work. A fur importer[13] had once offered[14] him a job as a driver. He would find him tomorrow and ask for the position[15]. He would be somebody in the world. He would . . .

1. respond to 對……有反應
2. impulse [ˋɪmpʌls] (n.)
   衝動;刺激
3. desperate [ˋdɛspərɪt] (a.)
   絕望的;險惡的
4. fate [feɪt] (n.) 命運
5. condition [kənˋdɪʃən] (n.)
   情境
6. conquer [ˋkɑːŋkər] (v.)
   征服
7. evil [ˋiːvəl] (n.) 邪惡;罪惡
8. eager [ˋiːgər] (a.)
   渴望於……
9. pursue [pərˋsuː] (v.) 追逐
10. solemn [ˋsɑːləm] (a.)
    神聖嚴肅的

Soapy suddenly felt a hand on his arm. He looked quickly around into the broad[16] face of a policeman.

"What are you doing here?" asked the officer.

"Nothing," said Soapy.

"Then come along," said the policeman.

"You're under arrest[17] for loitering[18]."

"Three months on the Island," said the Judge in the Police Court the next morning.

11. note [nout] (n.) 音符
12. revolution [ˌrevəˈluːʃən] (n.) 革命性巨變
13. importer [imˈpɔːrtər] (n.) 進口者
14. offer [ɑːfər] (v.) 提供
15. position [pəˈzɪʃən] (n.) 職位
16. broad [brɔːd] (a.) 寬的
17. under arrest 被逮捕
18. loiter [ˈlɔɪtər] (v.) 閒逛

A Match the sentence with the person who says it.

❶ Soapy

❷ A policeman

❸ The well-dressed man

❹ The pretty woman

❺ The judge

Ⓐ Three months on the Island.

Ⓑ If it's your umbrella, I hope you'll excuse me.

Ⓒ Sure, Mike, if you'll buy me a few drinks.

Ⓓ Well, why don't you call a policeman?

Ⓔ It must be one of those Yale students.

B Fill in the blanks with the given words.

gloomy   aggressive   vicious   ambitious

❶ Soapy took the umbrella from the man in the liquor store. _____

❷ Soapy decided to change his life outside the church. _____

❸ Soapy was mistaken for a Yale student. _____

❹ Soapy came on to the young woman. _____

C Choose the correct answer.

1 Why didn't the cop arrest Soapy for harassing the young woman?

(a) She pretended to know him.

(b) The cop was only interested in burglars.

(c) The cop was distracted by a traffic accident.

2 Why didn't the cop arrest Soapy for singing on the street?

(a) Because the cop liked the song Soapy was singing.

(b) Because the cop thought Soapy was a celebrating college student.

(c) Because the cop was a kind man.

D Rearrange the given words in correct order.

1 A large policeman with a stern expression _____

_____.

(against / the building / the wall / leaned / of)

2 Soapy walked along a street that was under construction and _____.

(open / the umbrella / into / threw / an / hole)

3 To his sudden horror, _____.

(had / how / he / terrible / realized / life / become / his)

The Life of O. Henry

O. Henry was actually born as William Sydney Porter in Greensboro, North Carolina. He moved out west, to Texas, when he was fifteen years old to work in a drugstore and then on a ranch[1].

He was an avid[2] reader, and because of this influence[3], he tried to start a magazine. However, it soon failed. He then found work as a reporter for a newspaper in a large Texan city: the Houston Post.

He got married and had a daughter. However, he was convicted of[4] embezzling[5] money from the newspaper, and was sent to prison in Ohio. There was much debate[6] over his actual guilt. While in prison, he started to write short stories to support[7] his family.

---

1. ranch [ræntʃ] (n.) 飼養場；大牧場
2. avid [`ævɪd] (a.) 渴望的；熱情的
3. influence [`ɪnfluəns] (n.) 影響
4. be convicted of 被判有……罪
5. embezzle [ɪm`bezəl] (v.) 盜用；侵占
6. debate [dɪ`beɪt] (n.) 爭議；辯論
7. support [sə`pɔːrt] (v.) 支持

After leaving prison, he changed his name to O. Henry and moved to New York. He lived there for eight years. He wrote hundreds of short stories, many of them based in places he had lived in or visited.

His stories can be divided[8] by the regions[9] of their settings[10] : South, West, Latin America, and New York. However, he is most famous for his short stories that feature[11] life in New York City. These stories usually focus on[12] the lives of ordinary[13] people who experience ironic or circumstantial[14] twist of fate at the end of the story. These surprise endings illustrate[15] the random and unexpected events in life that bring out the best and worst of our human traits[16].

---

8. divide [dɪˋvaɪd] (v.) 分割；區分
9. region [ˋriːdʒən] (n.) 地區
10. setting [ˋsetɪŋ] (n.) 環境；背景
11. feature [ˋfiːtʃər] (v.) 以……為特色
12. focus on 注重於……
13. ordinary [ˋɔːrdəneri] (a.) 平凡平庸的
14. circumstantial [ˌsɜːrkəmˋstænʃəl] (a.) 詳細的；與情況有關的
15. illustrate [ˋɪləstreɪt] (v.) 描繪；說明
16. trait [treɪt] (n.) 特點

After Twenty Years

二十年後

Chapter One

30

A 20-year Appointment

The policeman made his rounds[1] up the avenue in an impressive[2] way. His impressiveness was habitual[3] and not for show, for there were few people around. The time was barely[4] 10 o'clock at night, but chilly gusts of wind with a taste of [5] rain in them had driven most people indoors.

The cop tested doors as he went to make sure they were locked[6]. He twirled his club like a master in martial arts[7]. He turned now and then to cast[8] his watchful[9] eye down the broad street. The officer, with his large form[10] and confident walk, made a fine picture of a guardian[11] of the peace[12].

1. make one's rounds
   巡迴；巡視
2. impressive [ɪmˋprɛsɪv] (a.)
   威嚴的
3. habitual [həˋbɪtʃuəl] (a.)
   出於慣性的
4. barely [ˋbɛrli] (adv.)
   剛好地
5. a taste of 些許的
6. lock [lɑːk] (v.) 上鎖

His assigned[13] area was one where most shops closed early at night. Now and then, a person might see the lights of a liquor store or an all-night small restaurant, but the majority of[14] the doors belonged to[15] business owners who had already gone home several hours ago.

7. martial art 武術
8. cast [kæst] (v.) 投射
   cast one's eye (over)
   匆匆掃視
9. watchful [ˋwɑːtʃfəl] (a.)
   戒備的；注意的
10. form [fɔːrm] (n.) 體態
11. guardian [ˋgɑːrdiən] (n.)
    管理員；守護者
12. peace (n.) 和平
13. assigned [əˋsaɪn] (a.)
    被指派的；被分配的
14. the majority of 大多數
15. belong to 屬於

🎧 31

About halfway down one block, the policeman suddenly slowed his pace[1]. In the doorway[2] of a dark entrance[3] to a hardware store, a man leaned. He had an unlit[4] cigarette in his mouth. As the policeman walked up to him, the loiterer[5] spoke quickly.

1. pace [peɪs] (n.) 腳步
2. doorway [ˋdɔːrweɪ] (n.) 出入口；門口
3. entrance [ˋentrəns] (n.) 入口
4. unlit [ˋlɪt] (a.) 未點燃的
5. loiter [ˋlɔɪtər] (v.) 閒晃
6. reassuringly [ˌriːəˋʃʊrɪŋli] (adv.) 可靠地；安慰地

7. sound [saʊnd] (v.) 聽起來
8. make certain 確定
9. tear down 拆除
10. strike a match 點火柴
11. pale [peɪl] (a.) 蒼白的
12. square-jawed (a.) 方顎的
13. keen [kiːn] (a.) 銳利的
14. scar [skɑːr] (n.) 傷疤

"It's all right, officer," he said, reassuringly[6].

"I'm just waiting for a friend. We made an appointment twenty years ago. Sounds[7] a little funny to you, doesn't it? Well, I'll explain it to you if you'd like to make certain[8] everything is all right. About that long ago, there used to be a restaurant where this store stands —"Big Joe' Brady's restaurant."

"Until five years ago," said the policeman. "It was torn down[9] then."

The man in the doorway struck a match[10] and lit his cigarette. The light showed a pale[11], square-jawed[12] face with keen[13] eyes and a little white scar[14] near his right eyebrow. He had a diamond pin in his scarf.

✔ *Check Up*

True or False.

a The man was waiting for his friend to keep an appointment.____

b The man gave a gentle impression.____

Ans: a T b F

🎧 32

"Twenty years ago tonight," said the man, "I ate here at 'Big Joe' Brady's with Jimmy Wells, my best friend and the best guy in the world. He and I were raised[1] here in New York, just like two brothers, together. I was eighteen, and Jimmy was twenty. The next morning, I was to go out to the West to make my fortune[2]. You couldn't have dragged[3] Jimmy out of New York; he thought it was the only place on earth[4].

Well, we agreed that night that we would meet here again exactly twenty years from that date and time, no matter what our conditions might be or from what distance[5] we might have to come.

1. raise [reɪz] (v.) 扶養
2. make one's fortune
   賺大錢
3. drag [dræg] (v.) 拖拉
4. on earth 世界上
5. distance [`dɪstəns] (n.) 距離
6. figure [`fɪgjər] (v.) 認為
7. destiny [`destɪni] (n.) 命運
8. work out 發展；成功
9. rather [`ræðər] (adv.)
   頗；相當地
10. hear from 聽聞……的消息

We figured[6] that in twenty years, each of us ought to have our destiny[7] worked out[8] and our fortunes made, whatever they were going to be."

"It sounds pretty interesting," said the policeman. "But it seems to me that you have had a rather[9] long time between meetings. Haven't you heard from[10] your friend since you left?"

33

"Well, yes, for a time[1] we wrote to each other," said the man. "But after a year or two, we lost track of [2] each other. You see, the West is a pretty[3] big place, and I kept moving around pretty frequently[4]. But I know Jimmy will meet me here if he's alive[5], for he always was the most loyal[6] friend in the world. He'll never forget. I came a thousand miles to stand in this door tonight, and it's worth[7] it if my old friend turns up[8]."

The waiting man pulled out[9] an expensive watch. Small diamonds in the wristband[10] sparkled[11] in the faint[12] light of a street lamp.

1. for a time 一陣子
2. lose track of 失去聯絡
3. pretty [`prɪti] (adv.) 相當地
4. frequently [`friːkwəntli] (adv.) 時常地
5. alive [ə`laɪv] (a.) 活著的
6. loyal [`lɔɪəl] (a.) 忠實的
7. be worth 值得……
8. turn up 出現
9. pull out 拔出
10. wristband [`rɪstbænd] (n.) 錶帶
11. sparkle [`spɑːrkl] (v.) 閃耀
12. faint [feɪnt] (a.) 昏暗的

"Three minutes to ten," he announced. "It was exactly ten o'clock when we parted[13] here at the restaurant door, twenty years ago."

"You did pretty well out in the West, didn't you?" asked the policeman.

"You bet[14]! I hope Jimmy has done half as well. He was a little lazy, though, even if he was a good fellow[15]. I've had to compete[16] with some very smart men to make my fortune. A man can get lazy in New York. It takes the West to put a competitive[17] edge[18] on him."

13. part [pɑːrt] (v.) 離開
14. You bet! 你說對了！
15. fellow [`felou] (n.) 傢伙

16. compete [kəm`piːt] (v.) 競爭
17. competitive [kəm`petətɪv] (a.) 有競爭力的
18. put an edge on 把……磨鋒利

Check Up

What's the wrong answer?

ⓐ The man seemed to be successful in the West.
ⓑ Jimmy was a very faithful friend to the man.
ⓒ The man was afraid Jimmy would forget the appointment.

Ans: c

34

The policeman twirled his club and took a step or two.

"I'll be on my way. Hope your friend comes around all right. Are you going to leave if he doesn't show up[1] exactly on time[2]?"

"No way[3]!" said the other. "I'll give him half an hour at least[4]. If Jimmy is alive on Earth, he'll be here by that time. So long, officer."

"Good night, sir," said the policeman, passing down the street, trying doors as he went.

1. show up 出現
2. on time 準時
3. no way 不可能
4. at least 至少
5. slight [slaɪt] (a.) 微小的
6. collar [`kɑːlər] (n.) 領口
7. keep an appointment
   信守約定
8. boyhood [`bɔɪhʊd] (n.)
   少年時代
9. ridiculous [rɪ`dɪkjuləs] (a.)
   荒謬的

There was now a slight[5], cold rain falling, and the wind had become stronger, so now it blew steadily. The few pedestrians on the streets hurried gloomily and silently along with their coat collars[6] turned high and their hands in their pockets.

And in the door of the hardware store, the man who had come a thousand miles to keep an appointment[7] with his boyhood[8] friend, no matter how ridiculous[9] it seemed, smoked his cigarette and waited.

True or False.

[a] The man asked the policeman to find his old friend. ____
[b] The man would wait for his friend until at least 10:30. ____

35

About twenty minutes he waited, and then a tall man in a long overcoat[1], with the collar turned up to his ears, hurried across from the opposite side of the street. He went directly to the waiting man.

"Is that you, Bob?" he asked, doubtfully[2].

"Is that you, Jimmy Wells?" cried the man in the door.

"Incredible[3]!" exclaimed[4] the new arrival[5], grasping[6] both the other's hands with his own.

"It's Bob, true to[7] his word[8]. I was certain I'd find you here if you were still in existence[9]. Well, well, well! — twenty years is a long time. The old restaurant is gone[10], Bob; I wish it had lasted[11] so we could have had another dinner there. How has the West treated[12] you, old man?"

1. **overcoat** [ˈouvərkout] (n.)
   大衣
2. **doubtfully** [dautfəli] (adv.)
   懷疑地
3. **incredible** [ɪnˈkredɪbəl] (a.)
   不可置信的
4. **exclaim** [ɪkˈskleɪm] (v.)
   大叫
5. **arrival** [əˈraɪvəl] (n.)
   到達的人
6. **grasp** [græsp] (v.) 緊抓

"Excellent; it has given me everything I asked it for. You've changed lots, Jimmy. I never thought you were so tall. You're quite a few centimeters taller than I remember."

"Oh, I grew a bit after I was twenty."

7. true to 忠實於
8. one's word 諾言
9. in existence 活著
10. be gone 消失
11. last [læst] (v.) 持續存在
12. treat [triːt] (v.) 對待

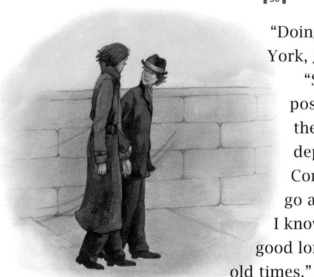

36

"Doing well in New York, Jimmy?"

"So-so. I have a position in one of the city departments[1]. Come on, Bob; we'll go around to a place I know of and have a good long talk about old times."

The two men started up the street, arm in arm[2]. The man from the West had become excited by success. He was beginning to tell the story of his career[3]. The other, hidden[4] in his overcoat, listened with interest.

1. department [dɪˋpɑːrtmənt] (n.) 部門
2. arm in arm 臂膀挽著臂膀
3. career [kəˋrɪr] (n.) 事業
4. hidden [ˋhɪdn] (a.) 隱藏的
5. brilliant [ˋbrɪljənt] (a.) 亮的
6. electric light (n.) 電燈
7. look upon (v.) 看
8. release [rɪˋliːs] (v.) 鬆開
9. snap [snæp] (v.) 厲聲說

At the corner stood a drugstore, brilliant[5] with electric lights[6]. When they came into this light, each of them turned at the same time to look upon[7] the other's face.

The man from the West stopped suddenly and released[8] his arm.

"You're not Jimmy Wells," he snapped[9]. "Twenty years is a long time, but not long enough to change a man's nose from long and thin to short and wide."

✓ Check Up

The man from the West was upset when he found out that _____.

　ⓐ the other was the owner of the drugstore
　ⓑ the other was not his friend Jimmy
　ⓒ the other had plastic surgery

Ans: b

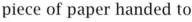

37

"But it sometimes changes a good man into a bad one," said the tall man. "You've been under arrest for ten minutes, 'Silky' Bob. The Chicago Police Department thought you would come to New York. They want to have a chat with[1] you. You'll come quietly, won't you? That's the smart thing to do. Now, before we go on to the police station, here's a note[2] I was asked to[3] hand you. You may read it here at the window. It's from Police Officer Wells."

The man from the West unfolded[4] the little piece of paper handed to

him. His hand was steady[5] when he began to read, but it trembled[6] a little by the time he had finished. The note was rather short.

---

1. have a chat with
   和……聊天
2. note [nout] (n.) 字條
3. be asked to 被要求做……
4. unfold [ʌnˈfould] (v.) 打開

5. steady [ˈstedi] (a.) 穩定
6. tremble [ˈtrembl̩] (v.) 顫抖
7. appointed [əˈpɔɪntɪd] (a.)
   約定的

Bob,

I was at the appointed[7] place on time. When you struck the match to light your cigar, I saw it was the face of the man wanted[8] in Chicago. Somehow[9] I couldn't do it myself, so I went around and got[10] a plain clothes[11] man to do the job.

Jimmy

8. wanted [ˈwɑːntɪd] (a.)
   被通緝的

9. somehow [ˈsʌmhaʊ] (adv.)
   不知怎麼地

10. get sb to 使某人去⋯⋯

11. plain clothes
    [pleɪn kloʊðz] (n.) (a.)
    便衣警察；普通穿著的

Check Up

What's the wrong answer?

[a] The man from the West was on the wanted list in Chicago.
[b] Jimmy went to the appointed place to meet his friend.
[c] The man in a long overcoat was Jimmy's friend.

Ans: c

105

A Choose the correct answer.

1 What is this story about?

(a) Boyhood friends who promised to meet again after 20 years.

(b) Two strangers who took very different paths in life.

(c) A policeman who finally arrested the man he has been hunting for 20 years.

2 Who is Jimmy Wells?

(a) A big time criminal who made his fortune in the West.

(b) The policeman at the beginning of the story.

(c) The man in the overcoat who greeted Bob on the street.

B Fill in the blanks according to the story.

note	jewelry	club	fortune

1 The plainclothes man gave 'Silky' Bob a _____ from Jimmy Wells.

2 Bob went out to the West to make his _____.

3 The man in the doorway had expensive _____ that glittered in the light.

4 The policeman twirled his _____ and walked away down the street.

Appendixes

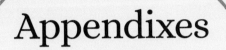

1 Basic Grammar

要增強英文閱讀理解能力，應練習找出英文的主結構。
要擁有良好的英語閱讀能力，首先要理解英文的段落結構。

「英文的閱讀理解從「分解文章」開始」

英文的文章是以「有意義的詞組」（指帶有意義的語句）所構成的。用（／）符號來區別各個意義語塊，請試著掌握其中的意義。

He knew / that she told a lie / at the party.

他知道　　　　　她說了謊　　　　在舞會上

As she was walking / in the garden, / she smelled /

當她行走　　　　　花園中　　　　聞到了

something wet.

濕潤的氣味

一篇文章，要分成幾個有意義的詞組？

可放入（／）符號來區隔有意義詞組的地方，一般是在（1）「主詞＋動詞」之後；（2）and 和 but 等連接詞之前；（3）that、who 等關係代名詞之前；（4）副詞子句的前後，會用（／）符號來區隔。初學者可能在一篇文章中畫很多（／）符號，但隨著閱讀實力的提升，（／）會減少。時間一久，在不太複雜的文章中即使不畫（／）符號，也能一眼就理解整句的意義。

使用（／）符號來閱讀理解英語篇章
1. 能熟悉英文的句型和構造。
2. 可加速閱讀速度。

該方法對於需要邊聽理解的英文聽力也有很好的效果。
從現在開始，早日丟棄過去理解文章的習慣吧！

以直接閱讀理解的方式，重新閱讀《歐·亨利短篇小說》

從原文中摘錄一小段。以具有意義的詞組將文章做斷句區分，重新閱讀並做理解練習。

In a little district west of Washington Square, / the street
have run crazy //
在一個西邊華盛頓的一個轄區　　　　　　　　　　／街道規劃古怪

and have broken the district / into strange shapes. //
將轄區分割為　　　　　　　　／奇特的形狀

This district is called Greenwich Village. //
轄區名為格林威治村

An artist once discovered / a valuable feature of this district. //
曾經有位藝術家發現　　　/ 轄區珍貴的特點

On such streets, / it is very likely / that a bill collector with a bill for
在這樣的街道　/ 很容易　　　/ 要討顏料畫紙油畫布的債主會迷路

paints, paper, and canvas would get lost

while trying to find the address of the artist / who owes him money! //
當尋找藝術家住處時　　　　　　　　　/ 欠他錢的人

So, artists came in large numbers / to quaint, old Greenwich Village.//
因此大批藝術家湧入　　　　　/ 古怪老舊的格林威治村

At the top of an ugly, three-story brick apartment building, //
在一棟難看三層磚瓦的公寓建築中

Sue and Johnsy rented a small studio. //
蘇和瓊西租了一間小套房

Sue was from Maine; / Johnsy was from California. //
蘇是從緬因州來的　　　/ 瓊西是從加州來的

They had met at a small cafe on Eighth street / and found that their //
她們在第八大道上的一間小咖啡館裡相遇　　/ 發現彼此
tastes in art, food, and clothes were so much alike //
在藝術食物衣著的品味很相像

that they decided to rent a place together. //
便決定一起租下住處

That was in May. //
於五月時

In November, a cold, unseen stranger / whom the doctors called
十一月　　　　一位冷酷生面孔的陌生人 / 被醫生稱為肺炎

touching people here and there / with his icy fingers. //
四處侵襲人們　　　　　　　/ 以它冰冷的手指

A small woman with blood thinned / by the warm California sun //
一位年輕女孩血裡流著　　　　　/ 溫暖的加州陽光

was no match / for the tough and deadly illness. //
無法抵抗　 / 難纏致命的疾病

Johnsy got pneumonia, / and it made her very ill. //
瓊西得了肺炎　　　　/ 這使得她感到病懨懨

She lay, / hardly moving / on her iron-framed bed, //
她臥躺 / 難以移動　　/ 在她鐵床架的床上

looking through the small window / at the brick wall of the building
從小小的窗望出　　　　　　　/ 在隔壁棟磚牆中
next door.//

One morning, / the busy doctor invited Sue / into the hallway. //
一早　　　　/ 忙碌的醫師來拜訪蘇　　　/ 在走廊上

His eyes were sad / under his bushy gray eyebrows. //
他眼神悲傷　　 / 在他濃密灰白眉毛下

"She has one chance in / —let us say, ten,"/ he said, //
她有活下去的機會　　　 / 就說十分之一好了 / 他說

as he looked at his clinical thermometer. //
當他看了溫度計

"And that chance depends / on her will to live. //
這機會取決於　　　　　 / 她的生存意志

Guide to Listening Comprehension

 When listening to the story, use some of the techniques shown below. If you take time to study some phonetic characteristics of English, listening will be easier.

Get in the flow of English.

English creates a rhythm formed by combinations of strong and weak stress intonations. Each word has its particular stress that combines with other words to form the overall pattern of stress or rhythm in a particular sentence.

When you are speaking and listening to English, it is essential to get in the flow of the rhythm of English. It takes a lot of practice to get used to such a rhythm. So, you need to start by identifying the stressed syllable in a word.

Listen for the strongly stressed words and phrases.

In English, key words and phrases that are essential to the meaning of a sentence are stressed louder. Therefore, pay attention to the words stressed with a higher pitch. When listening to an English recording for the first time, what matters most is to listen for a general understanding of what you hear. Do not try to hear every single word. Most of the unstressed words are articles or auxiliary verbs, which don't play an important role in the general context. At this level, you can ignore them.

Pay attention to liaisons.

In reading English, words are written with a space between them. There isn't such an obvious guide when it comes to listening to English. In oral English, there are many cases when the sounds of words are linked with adjacent words.

For instance, let's think about the phrase "**take off**," which can be used in "take off your clothes." "Take off your clothes" doesn't sound like [teɪk ɔːf] with each of the words completely and clearly separated from the others. Instead, it sounds as if almost all the words in context are slurred together, [ˈteɪkɔːf], for a more natural sound.

Shadow the voice of the native speaker.

Finally, you need to mimic the voice of the native speaker. Once you are sure you know how to pronounce all the words in a sentence, try to repeat them like an echo. Listen to the book again, but this time you should try a fun exercise while listening to the English.

This exercise is called "shadowing." The word "shadow" means a dark shade that is formed on a surface. When used as a verb, the word refers to the action of following someone or something like a shadow. In this exercise, pretend you are a parrot and try to shadow the voice of the native speaker.

Try to mimic the reader's voice by speaking at the same speed, with the same strong and weak stresses on words, and pausing or stopping at the same points.

Experts have already proven this technique to be effective. If you practice this shadowing exercise, your English speaking and listening skills will improve by leaps and bounds. While shadowing the native speaker, don't forget to pay attention to the meaning of each phrase and sentence.

Step 1

Listen to what you want to shadow many times. Start out by just trying to shadow a few words or a sentence.

Step 2

Mimic the CD out loud. You can shadow everything the speaker says as if you are singing a round, or you also can speak simultaneously with the recorded voice of the native speaker.

Step 3

As you practice more, try to shadow more. For instance, shadow a whole sentence or paragraph instead of just a few words.

以下為《歐・亨利短篇小説》各章節的前半部。一開始若能聽清楚發音，之後就沒有聽力的負擔。先聽過摘錄的章節，之後再反覆聆聽括弧內單字的發音，並仔細閱讀各種發音的説明。以下都是以英語的典型發音為基礎，所做的簡易説明，即使這裡未提到的發音，也可以配合音檔反覆聆聽，如此一來聽力必能更上層樓。

Chapter One page 16–17 🎧 38

(**1**) ( ) little district west of Washington Square, the streets have run crazy and (**2**) ( ) the district into strange shapes. This district is called Greenwich Village. An artist once discovered a valuable feature of this district. On such streets, (**3**) ( ) very likely that a bill collector with a bill for paints, paper, and canvas (**4**) get lost while trying to find the address of the artist who owes him money! So, artists came in large numbers to quaint, old Greenwich Village.

At the top of an ugly, three-story brick (**5**) ( ), Sue and Johnsy rented a small studio. Sue was from Maine; Johnsy was from California. They had met at a small cafe on Eighth street and found that their tastes in art, food, and clothes were so much (**6**) that they decided to rent a place together. That was in May.

❶ **In a:** 和 a 一起發音時，子音 [n] 會與母音 [ə] 產生連音，唸成 [ɪnə]。

❷ **have broken:** have 單獨發音時為 [hæv]，[v] 為開口音，但 broken 的 [b] 為閉口音，故唸時省略 [v] 的音。

❸ **it is:** it 與 is 一起發音時，子音 [t] 會與母音 [ɪ] 產生連音，唸成 [ɪtɪz]。

❹ **would:** would 在文中只需以低調帶過，因為此字僅具輔助文意。

❺ **apartment building:** apartment 最後的 [t] 在與 building 一起發音時省略。

❻ **alike:** alike 重音在 [ə] 之後。

In November, a cold, unseen (❶) whom the doctors called pneumonia came to Greenwich Village, touching people here and there (❷) ( ) icy fingers. A small woman with blood thinned by the warm California sun was no match for the tough and deadly illness. Johnsy got pneumonia, and it made her very ill. She lay, hardly moving on her iron-framed (❸), looking through the small window at the brick wall of the building (❹) ( ).

One morning, the busy doctor invited Sue into the hallway. His eyes were sad under his bushy gray eyebrows.

"She has one chance in – (❺) ( ) ( ), ten," he said, as he looked at his clinical thermometer. "And that chance depends on her will to live. Sometimes when people (❻) ( ) trying to live, it doesn't matter what medicines I give. Your friend has decided, for some reason, that she is not going to get well."

❶ **stranger:** 無聲子音 p、t、k 接在 s- 之後會成為有聲子音,轉變為 [b]、[d]、[g]。

❷ **with his:** with 的 [h] 和 his 的 [h] 是相同子音,故兩個相同子音同時出現,第一個子音需被省略。

❸ **bed:** bed 的 [b] 發音方式為氣流阻塞於雙唇,聲帶震動發出類似注音「ㄅ」的音。

❹ **next door:** next 單獨發音時需發出 [t] 的音,但與 door 一起唸時發成 [neksdɔ:r]。

❺ **let us say:** let 的 [t] 與 us 的 [ə] 為子母音連音,us [s] 和 say [s] 則是子音相同省略前子音,故唸成 [letəseɪ]。

❻ **give up:** give 的 [v] 與 up 的 [ʌ] 為子母音連音,原則唸成 [gɪvʌp]。

4

Listening Comprehension

 A Listen to the CD and choose the correct definition of character.

a Behrman   b Johnsy   c Soapy   d 'Silky' Boy

❶ _____ ❷ _____ ❸ _____ ❹ _____

B Listen to the CD, write down the question and choose the correct answer.

❶ _____?

    (a) Breaking a shop window.

    (b) Loitering on the streets.

    (c) Making noise and bothering pedestrians.

❷ _____?

    (a) Giving Johnsy good nutrition and proper care.

    (b) Getting Johnsy interested in life again.

    (c) Being nice to old Behrman.

🎧 42 **C** Listen to the CD, write down the sentences and circle either true or false.

T F **1**
....

T F **2**
....

T F **3**
....

T F **4**
....

🎧 43

D Listen to the CD and fill in the blanks.

1 Soapy _____ _____ a park bench in Madison Square.

2 Soapy _____ _____ eat a meal and not pay for it.

3 The church music helped Soapy decide to _____ his _____.

4 Bob did not _____ Jimmy as a _____ policeman.

5 Johnsy lay in her bed, _____ as a fallen _____.

6 Old Behrman _____ _____ when he heard about Johnsy.

歐・亨利（William S. Porter；"O. Henry"，1862–1910）是個美國短篇小說作家，擅於製造出人意料的結尾。本名為威廉・西德尼・波特，據說這名氣響亮的筆名也是他的貓的名字。

廉・西德尼・波特生於北卡羅來納州的格林斯伯勒（Greensboro），父親阿爾格農・西德尼・波特（Algernon Sidney Porter）是名外科醫生。威廉三歲時，母親感染肺結核病逝，他與父親遷居於祖母的家。

他熱愛閱讀，但 15 歲時離開學校，到叔叔的藥局當記帳員，接下來數年間從事數種工作，包括藥劑師、繪圖員、記者和出納員。1896 年，他因挪用公款被起訴，判五年徒刑。三年後的 1901 年 7 月 24 日，由於表現良好而被釋放。

服刑期間，他根據自身經歷開始書寫短篇小說。為了不讓讀者知道他在監獄受刑，他開始使用筆名「歐・亨利」。獲釋後他遷居紐約積極寫作，此十年間共寫了將近 300 篇短篇故事。

他著名的《最後一片葉子》（The Last Leaf）、《聖誕禮物》（The Gift of the Magi）和其他纖細敏感的著作，內容大多描述美國南方與紐約後街裡，窮苦百姓的生活悲歡。

歐・亨利的著作富含幽默、機智與渲染力，並展現他對人性心理感受的深刻見解。他精妙的構想、充滿巧思的劇情及出人意料的結尾，也彰顯他身為作家源源不絕的想像力。

〈最後一片葉子〉

　　故事背景設定在 1905 年紐約的格林威治村，以生動的開頭向讀者介紹畫家瓊西與她的新室友雕刻家蘇。兩位年輕藝術家共租一間公寓。冬日逼近，氣候轉寒，瓊西染上肺炎，儘管蘇持續照料，病情仍無好轉。她瀕臨死亡，失去了求生意志。瓊西躺在床上，盯著窗外磚牆上的長春藤蔓，相信最後一片葉子墜落之際，也就是她死亡之時。

　　然而，一位突如其來的英雄現身拯救了瓊西。年邁的貝爾曼先生是位不得志的畫家，也是她們的鄰居。因為想替垂死的瓊西找回求生意志，他與自己的病魔奮鬥，在暴風雨的夜晚，替外頭的藤蔓畫上一片永不會墜落的葉子。因為淋雨受寒，他得了肺炎去世了。但葉子給了瓊西希望，支撐她捱過病痛，而那片葉子也成為貝爾曼先生一直夢想繪畫出的傑作。

〈警察與讚美詩〉

　　〈警察與讚美詩〉以諷刺手法好心的流浪漢索匹如何進入監牢。天氣越發寒冷，因為擔心冬天的到來，索匹決定被捕入牢即為上策，他認為監獄是個可以溫暖安睡的地方。

〈二十年後〉

　　〈二十年後〉講述鮑伯與吉米兩位好友，約好 20 年後要再次相會於離別前一晚用餐的餐廳。他們設想，那時兩人的命運應已各自發展，並得到財富。在西部收穫成功的鮑伯，回到約定場所，等待吉米的出現。

蘇

　　我不過是一位窮苦的藝術家，與我的摯友瓊西居住在一塊兒。眼見天氣越漸寒冷，瓊西罹患了肺炎，而醫生卻沒給她生存下來的希望，這可真令我傷心。

瓊西

　　我感到病懨懨和疲倦，也知道自己就快死去，但我只想撐下去，直到看見長春藤的最後一葉落下，很快地，我的生命將會隨著葉落而結束。

貝爾曼

　　這是那門子的胡說八道呀？那女孩居然認為，從藤上落下葉子時，她就會跟著死去，簡直是瘋狂至極！我一定要採取一些行動，去保護那可憐的小東西。

索匹

　　嗯……我想，是時候來安排年度的冬季島嶼之旅了，那可不是加勒比海上的什麼島喔，而是紐約市旁邊那座監獄島嶼。我得想個法子，看要怎麼去那裡。

吉米

　　二十年啦！自從上次見我的童年玩伴到現在，已經這麼久了，但今晚我們將會再度碰頭，沒錯！正在二十年前告別的那家餐廳，現在則改成一家五金行。等等喔，有人在門口。

鮑伯

　　嘿！這裡！你認識有位叫做吉米威爾斯的人嗎？我晚上十點要在這裡與他見面，不知道他是否有所改變，我自己當然是不同於以往，而且我過得可好了。

最後一片葉子

[第一章] 肺炎來襲

p. 16-17 華盛頓西邊街區的小轄區內，街道規劃古怪，轄區被分割成奇特的形狀。此區稱為格林威治村，從前有一位藝術家發現了這村極珍貴的特色，那就是在這區域中，要是有債主上門，不管是討顏料、紙或是油畫布的錢，債主們都會迷路！因此，大批藝術家湧進了這古怪、老舊的格林威治村中。

在一難看的三層磚瓦公寓頂樓，蘇與瓊西租了一間小房間。蘇是緬因州人，瓊西是加州來的，她們在第八大道的小咖啡館相遇，發現彼此不管是在藝術、食物和衣著的品味上，都很相似，便在五月時決定一起租屋住在一塊。

p. 18-19

十一月時，一位冷酷隱形、被醫生喚作肺炎的外來客來到了格林威治村，用它冰冷的手指，四處侵襲人們。一位有著加州溫暖陽光血統的年輕女子，完全無法抵擋這難纏致命的疾病。瓊西患了肺炎，重病在床，無法起身，只能臥病在鐵框邊的床上，對著隔壁棟的磚牆小窗望過去。

一天早晨，忙碌的醫生將蘇叫到走廊上，他濃密灰白眉毛下的雙眼，充滿了悲傷。

「這樣說吧，她只有十分之一的生存機會。」醫生看著他的診療溫度計，接著說：「這機會取決於她的求生意志。有時候是人自己放棄了生存的機會，跟開什麼藥沒有關係。妳的朋友可能因為什麼原因而不想好起來。」

p. 20–21 「有什麼事讓她掛心的嗎？」醫生問。

「她……她想有一天能畫下那不勒斯港的景象。」蘇回答。

「畫畫？不是這些！我是說，她現在有沒有什麼比較嚴重的困擾，像是感情之類的？」

「男人？」蘇語帶嘲諷地回問道：「值得為男人死嗎？沒有這種事，醫生。」

「那好吧，她現在很虛弱，我會盡我所知的來治療她。但是，只要病人認為自己時日不多了，那藥效就會減半了。妳要是能讓她問起今年冬天的流行服飾，那我保證，她的機會不是一成，而是兩成了。」

醫生離開後，蘇走進工作室，等眼淚哭乾了，才拿起畫板，吹著一首輕快流行曲子的口哨，若無其事地走進瓊西的房間。

p. 22–23 瓊西面對窗子躺著，床單下的身子沒有動靜，蘇以為她睡著了，便停止吹口哨。

蘇拿出畫板，開始用鋼筆為雜誌故事畫插圖。年輕藝術家一定要透過替雜誌小故事畫插圖，才能找到真正通往藝術之路，就如同年輕作家必須寫，才能進入真正的文學一樣。

當她在為一位愛達荷州牛仔，勾勒一條講究的褲子和牛仔帽時，聽見了持續著的低沉聲音，便快步走向床邊。

瓊西睜大眼睛，正望著窗外數數——是倒數。

她說著：「十二，」過一會兒，「十一」，又「十」和「九」，接著「八」和「七」，幾乎是糊在一起唸的。

p. 24–25 蘇好奇地看向窗外，那裡有什麼東西好數的？不過是一片光禿陰鬱的後院，而在八公尺外的紅磚建物那頭，有一株半攀上磚牆的老長春藤蔓，被冷冽的秋風吹得落葉飄零。

蘇問道：「親愛的，妳在看什麼？」

「六，它們掉落得更快了，三天前，差不多還有一百呢，算得我都頭疼了。不過，現在簡單多了，瞧！又去掉一個，現在只剩五了。」瓊西低聲說著。

「親愛的，五什麼啊？告訴妳的小蘇。」

「長春藤上的葉子呀。等到最後一片葉子落下，我也要走了。三天前我就知道了，難道醫生沒跟妳說？」

p. 26–27 「噢，這什麼無稽之談啊，我沒聽過。」蘇挖苦道：「老長春藤的葉子，和妳的復原有什麼關係呀？況且妳一向很喜愛這棵老藤的，傻女孩。那個啊，醫生早上跟我說，妳痊癒的機率──他是怎麼說的呀──他說啊，機會是十比一呢！這簡直就好比人在紐約時，可以搭地鐵或是會路過新大樓的機會一樣嘛。現在喝點湯吧，然後讓小蘇回去繼續畫圖，這樣她才有法子將畫賣給編輯，然後為病懨懨的朋友買些葡萄酒，為貪心的自己買些豬排。」

「不用再買什麼酒了。」瓊西依然望向窗外的說：「又掉了一片，不！我不想喝湯，只剩下四片葉子了，天黑之前希望能夠看見最後一葉掉落，那時候我也要走了。」。

p. 28–29 「親愛的瓊西。」蘇對著她彎下身，說道：「妳能答應我，先閉上眼睛，不要看外面，直到我工作結束嗎？這些圖明天一定要交，而且我需要光線，要不然會把陰影一併畫上去。」

瓊西淡淡的回答：「你不能到另一個房間畫嗎？」

「我寧願在這兒陪著妳。還有，不要再去看那些愚蠢的長春藤葉子了。」

「那等妳畫完後，跟我說一聲。」瓊西閉上雙眼，一臉蒼白，身子動也不動，猶如倒下的雕像一般，她說道：「因為我想見到最後一片落葉，不過，我不想再等，不想再傷腦筋了，想放棄一切就這樣離去，就像那些可悲疲累的葉子們。」

「睡一下吧。」蘇說：「我該叫貝爾曼來當我西部礦工的模特兒了，馬上就回來，在我回來前別亂動喔。」

[第二章] 曠世巨作

p. 32-33 老貝爾曼是一位住在她們樓下的德國畫家，年逾六十，寬寬的頭蓄著滿腮的捲鬍子，就像米開朗基羅所創作的摩西的鬍子。他是藝術領域中的失敗者，畫了四十多年了，也沒有什麼代表作。他向來都準備好要畫出什麼大作的，卻不曾真正開始著手。幾年過去了，還是偶爾替廣告畫畫小圖罷了。

他為本地區付不起專業模特兒費用的年輕畫家們擔任模特兒，掙了一些錢。儘管他酒喝得很凶，他仍大談著終有一天會畫出大作。他是個很悍的小老頭，很看不慣別人的軟弱。他把自己比為鬥犬，保護著樓上那兩位年輕的藝術家。

p. 34-35 蘇在陰暗的小房間裡，找到了渾身酒味的貝爾曼。房間角落有一張置於畫架上的空白畫布，它等著被畫上第一筆成為鉅作，已經等了二十五年了。

蘇告訴他瓊西的想法，並說自己很害怕瓊西真的會虛弱得如葉子般落下。老貝爾曼的眼裡噙著淚水，口中喊著對這種愚蠢想法的不屑。

他吼道：「什麼！這世上哪有人會愚蠢到只因為藤葉落下就會死在？真沒聽過這種事，我不當妳的模特兒了，你怎麼會讓她有這種蠢想法呢？喔！可憐的瓊西小姐。」

「她病得很重，又虛弱。」蘇說：「發燒使她變得憂鬱，滿腦子怪誕的想法。貝爾曼先生，行，要是你不想替我擺姿勢，那就算了，不過我認為你真是個糟老頭呀。」

p. 36-37 「女人家就是女人家！」貝爾曼大聲說著：「誰說我不擺姿勢啦！就走吧，我跟妳去，半小時前我就準備好啦。老天啊！這個地方，不適合瓊西小姐這種好人躺在那裡生病，等哪一天我畫出曠世巨作，我們就通通離開這裡，老天，就這麼說好了！」

當他們上樓時，瓊西還在睡。蘇把窗簾整個拉下，示意貝爾曼去另一房間。他們從另一間房望出去，憂心地看著長春藤，彼此沈默了好一陣子。夾著雪的冰雨持續下著，穿著老舊藍衫的貝爾曼，擺出西部礦工的樣子坐下。

隔日，當蘇小睡一小時後醒來，她看到瓊西睜著呆滯死大的眼睛，瞪著拉下的綠色簾子。

p. 38–39「拉上來，我要看。」瓊西低聲地要求。

蘇滿臉倦容地答應了。但是，等等！經過整晚暴雨的摧殘，和陣陣強風的來襲後，磚牆上只剩下一片長春藤葉。這是藤上最後的一葉，根部仍然維持著深綠色，但葉稜已開始泛黃枯萎，勇敢地掛在離地面二十呎高的枝上。

「這是最後一片葉子，它一定會在今晚落下，我聽見風兒說，它今天就會掉落，而我也會跟著一起死去。」瓊西說道。

「親愛的！」蘇一邊把瓊西憔悴的臉龐靠向枕頭，一邊說道：「如果妳不替自己著想，那也替我想吧，我該怎麼辦？」

瓊西沒有回答。世上最孤獨的事，莫過於一個人已經準備好要走完人生最後的未知路程。這念頭佔據心中，愈來愈強烈，讓她與友誼和人世的聯繫漸行相遠。

p. 40–41 白天過去了，黃昏中牆上那片掛在枝頭上的孤獨長春藤葉，仍隱約可見。隨著夜晚的來臨，北風呼嘯，大雨打在窗戶上，雨水沿著窗簷低處流下。

當天光亮些後，瓊西無情地要求把窗簾拉上。

長春葉子還在那兒呢。她倚在床上，看了好一陣子，然後呼叫正在攪動瓦斯爐上雞湯的蘇。

129

「我一直都是個不聽話的女孩，蘇。好像有什麼讓最後一片葉子掛在那兒，告訴我我有多壞！想死，是一種罪惡。現在，妳能幫我拿些湯和加點酒的牛奶嗎？等等，堆些枕頭，好讓我能坐起來看妳做菜。」

　　一小時後，她説：「小蘇，有那麼一天我希望能夠畫下那不勒斯港的景象。」

p. 42　醫生下午看診結束後離開，蘇陪同他至走廊。

　　「有五成的機會。」醫生握住蘇纖細顫抖的手説：「好好照顧就會成功的。現在我該去看另一個樓下的病人，貝爾曼，我看他也是個藝術家吧，也患了肺炎，一個又老又虛弱的人。病情很嚴重，沒什麼希望了。不過他今天上醫院去了，想讓自己好過一點。」

　　隔天，醫生對蘇説：「她已脫離險境，妳成功了！現在就只需要營養與照料。」

　　當天下午，蘇來到瓊西躺臥的床邊，她正開心地織著一條用不到的正藍色羊毛圍巾。蘇環抱著瓊西，還有枕頭那些的。

p. 44-45　「我有事要跟妳説，小白鼠。」她説：「貝爾曼先生今天在醫院去世了，是肺炎。才病了兩天就走了。樓管第一天早晨發現他時，他在他樓下的房間裡無助痛苦，全身冰冷濕透。他們想不透他在這麼惡劣的天候裡，究竟是去了哪裡。」

　　「後來，他們看到一盞亮著的提燈，一節從他住處搬來的梯子，還有四處散落的畫筆，和混合著綠色與黃色的調色盤。親愛的，看看窗外牆上最後的一片長春藤葉，你沒想過為什麼當風吹來時，它都毫無動靜呢？喔，親愛的，那是貝爾曼的傑作呀！他在最後一片葉子落下的那天夜裡，畫了這一幅圖。」

了解故事背景：料想不到的人性

p. 48–49 儘管歐·亨利當然並沒有發明了短篇故事，但他卻完全掌握了短篇故事的型式，並精通創造出人意料結尾的技巧。他用故事鋪陳結局，一開始提供一些暗示與看似不重要的細節，但在結局揭曉後，這些小地方卻成為關鍵。如同〈最後一片葉子〉的故事中，讀者們從住在樓下的老藝術家為了救樓上女孩所做的事之中，看出了些線索。

我們知道老人等了大半輩子，就是為了畫出曠世巨作，但我們並不期待他達成理想，而一直到最後結尾，我們才了解到他真的做到了，但也同時因無私的善行而受到致命傷害。

歐·亨利擅長使讀者對故事產生一種設想，再用驚奇的結尾粉碎這些想像。就像〈最後一片葉子〉，結局並不是殘酷命運隨意擺布的結，反而是由出色的作者刻意所安排，以顯示出我們有時意志薄弱、愚蠢卻無私善良的天性。

警察與讚美詩

[第一章] 索匹的冬日計畫

p. 52–53 在紐約的麥迪遜廣場中，索匹在長椅上不安地動來動去；野雁在高空中鳴叫，往南方飛去；街上店櫥窗外，沒有皮草大衣的女人們，對待丈夫的態度忽然變得更溫和了。當看見這些景象時，便知道冬天來臨了。

一片枯葉落在索匹膝上，那是冬神捎來的名片，祂很好心地向麥迪遜居民預告自己即將蒞臨。名片經北風之手傳送到各個角落，這樣一來，收到的人便能做好準備迎接寒冬。

索匹明白是時候思考對付緊接而來的嚴寒天氣了，要如何才能保持溫暖呢？該睡哪裡？這也是為什麼他在長椅上踟躕不安的原因。

p. 54–55 索匹對於今年過冬沒太大野心，也沒想過乘船到地中海度假，相反地，他只想在布萊克威爾斯島度過這一季。在那裡，每天都會有三頓熱騰騰的飯，晚上也會有溫暖的被窩，而且還有一起過冬的好夥伴。索匹的夢想就僅只於此了。

數個冬季以來，索匹都是在布萊克威爾斯島的監獄度過的。

當他好命的鄰居計畫前往陽光普照的南方景點遊玩時，他也正籌畫如何住進布萊克威爾監獄。

冬天到來了，前一晚的寒冷，讓索匹塞了三層週日報紙都不夠暖，他在古老廣場中的噴泉長椅上，冷到無法入睡。

p. 56–57 今天索匹滿腦子都在想著島嶼。他不願意尋求施捨，在他心中，法制體系比慈善機構來得好多了。雖然到處都有民間或宗教團體可以幫助他，不過在他有骨氣的想法裡，施捨總是要付出代價。每一次有人提供免費東西時，他的自尊就會感覺受損。除此之外，要是有人給他床睡，他就一定要先洗澡；要是他拿了麵包，施捨者就又要問一堆私人問題。

「這我才不幹呢！」索匹對於尋求慈善機構的協助，興趣缺缺，他心想：「法律有一定的規則可遵循，也不會涉及個人私事。」

p. 58–59 索匹鐵了心要前往布萊克威爾斯島，他得想想要怎麼去。有許多辦法都可行，而最愉快的方式，就是在一間豪華昂貴的餐廳享用霸王餐。如此一來，警察就會來將他帶走，法官會賜予他通往島嶼待上至少整個冬季的票券。

下定決心後，索匹從長椅上起身，走出廣場，穿越百老匯與第五大道交接的十字路口，到達百老匯。最後，他站在一家展示許多美味餐點的豪華餐廳外頭。

索匹對於自己的上半身，可是很有信心：鬍子刮得乾淨的白淨臉龐，外套也不錯，還打著前幾個禮拜感恩節時一位教會女士所送的新領帶。

p. 60–61 要是能順利進入餐廳坐下來，計畫就會成功。當他點菜單上最高價的餐點，外加一瓶上等好酒與高級雪茄時，侍者也不會看見他的下半身。

「我要來隻烤鴨。」索匹想。他知道自己付不出費用的話，餐廳老闆一定會想辦法對付他，而這一餐，將會送他踏上快樂的冬日旅程。

索匹暗自竊喜，然而他腳才剛要踏進餐廳時，就被領班瞧見。領班狐疑地上下打量索匹，看見他的老舊磨損的褲子和破鞋。索匹忽然感覺肩膀被幾個大漢一推，就這樣被趕了出來。

他走出百老匯，前往夢中島嶼的方法，看起來是與食物無關了。他得想想別的辦法，好往寒冬避風港去。

p. 62–63 在第六大道的轉角處，一大片的玻璃櫥窗吸引了索匹的目光，耶誕燈飾與精緻的產品陳列，真是賞心悅目極了。他撿拾起一顆石頭，往玻璃窗砸去。

民眾向轉角跑去，站最前頭的是一位警察。索匹手插著口袋，靜靜地站著，他一看到警徽，就笑了起來。

「砸玻璃的人在哪裡？」警察大聲問道。

「你不覺得我跟這事有關嗎？」索匹友好地說，彷彿在迎接自己的好運氣。

警察壓根不相信他是嫌疑犯。誰會在砸玻璃後還留在原地與他談話？一般早就開溜了。這時，警察遠遠看見街道那邊有個人急跑著要上車，他便掏出緊棍，跑去追那位不幸的市民了。失敗了兩次，索匹悻悻然地離開。

p. 64–65 對街有一家不太起眼的餐館，常客通常是那些食量大而預算少的人。這裡碗盤大，空氣濁；濃湯淡，桌巾薄。索匹走入店中，沒有人注意到他的舊鞋和破褲。他坐定位後，吃了一大塊牛排、煎餅、甜甜圈，還有一小塊烤派。用餐結束後，他告訴侍者，自己一毛錢也沒有，又說：「趕快張羅一下叫警察吧，別讓一位紳士等太久喔。」

「叫警察，門都沒有！」一位粗聲粗氣、雙眼漲紅的侍者說道。他呼叫另一個塊頭更大的侍者：「嘿，過來！」

那兩位侍者將索匹丟出店外，讓他的左身摔在堅硬的地板上。他慢慢地爬起來，檢查看有沒有骨折。他拍落衣服上的沙子，慶幸自己沒受什麼大傷。

想遭逮捕，像是個遙不可及的夢，這島就像個到不了的仙境啊。

在隔壁過兩個門的藥房外站著一位警察，他邊笑著，邊往著街走下去。

[第二章] 索匹注定要失敗

p. 68–69 索匹閒逛了五個街區後，才鼓起勇氣重施故技。這次他發現了一個必定會成功的機會，有一位年輕漂亮的女子站在櫥窗外，充滿興味地看著咖啡杯與銀器，而就在兩公尺遠的距離外，有一位神情嚴峻的警察正斜倚在牆邊。

索匹計畫調戲女子，就可以以騷擾的名義被逮捕。女子看起來就知道是出身良好，而他要裝成醉漢，那位嚴厲的警察一定會抓住他，這樣他很快就能前往島嶼上的溫暖巢窩，還有一天三餐的保障。

索匹拉緊領帶，並把褲子弄得舊舊亂亂的。他裝出輕佻挑釁的表情，走向年輕女子的身邊。

p. 70–71 他試著和女子有眼神接觸，在說話之前並大聲地清了清喉嚨。他對女子說了各種搭訕的話，有些話簡直是略帶了冒犯意味。索匹眼角瞥見到警察正盯著自己看。

　女子移動了幾步，繼續看著展示的咖啡杯具。他大膽地向前跟進，站到她身旁說：「來嘛，茉莉，不想跟我喝一杯嗎？」

　　警察仍在旁看著，被騷擾的女子只需舉起一根手指叫警察過來，索匹就能夠踏上島嶼之路了，他已經感受到警局的溫暖了。

　　突然，女子轉過身，抓住他的外套袖子，開心地說：「當然想囉，麥克！要是你請我喝飲料，我會跟你聊聊的，不過警察正看著呢。」

p. 72–73 年輕女子緊挽著他手臂，如同長春藤攀附著橡樹一樣。索匹喪氣地走過警察身邊，看來他還是逃不過這寒冷、寂寞的自由。

　　到了街口轉角，他甩開了女子的手溜走了。他在一區停了下來，他知道這一帶在晚上時，人們會愈顯得逍遙有活力。女人穿著皮草，男人穿著高級的冬大衣，開心地穿梭在冷冽空氣中。

　　忽然，一陣恐懼侵襲索匹，他猜想自己是否遭受魔咒，否則怎麼會無法被逮捕。這想法使他有些卻步。就在這時，他遇到一位站在燈火通明戲院外的警官，這又給了他一個被逮捕的靈感——妨礙社會秩序。

　　他開始在人行道上，以最刺耳的聲音，大聲胡言亂語、跳舞、吼叫，發瘋似大喊，並盡其所能地去騷擾路人。

p. 76–77 警察快速地轉動警棍並轉開身背對索匹，對著市民說：「這一定是耶魯大學的學生，在慶祝他們打敗哈特福德大學，贏得了足球比賽啦。他是很吵，不過不會鬧事的。我們有收到指示，不管他們就是了。」

再沒有比這更悶的事了，索匹停止了吵鬧。難道真的沒有警察會逮捕他嗎？在他心裡，那個島嶼就像個到達不了的天堂。他扣上外套抵禦寒風，向街頭走去。

透過洋酒商店的窗子，他看見一位穿著入時的男士買了一瓶酒，這位男士進店前，放了一把絲製的雨傘在店門口。索匹踏入店裡頭，將傘拿走，然後緩步地離開。這時，那位穿著體面的男士急忙地追上來，理直氣壯的說：「那是我的傘。」

p. 76-77 「喔，是嗎？」索匹盡其所能裝出卑劣模樣，諷刺地說：「既然如此，你何不叫警察，沒錯！我拿了你的傘，叫條子過來啊，轉角那裡有一個。」

雨傘主人慢下腳步，索匹也一樣，心想不會又失敗了吧。警官好奇地看著這兩個人。

「當然，這傘是……你知道的，誤會常就這樣發生，我……如果這是你的傘，我希望你能諒解，今早我在餐廳裡撿到這傘，如果你認為這是你的，那你何不……」雨傘主人說。

「當然了，這是我的傘！」索匹邪惡地說著。

雨傘前主人離開了，而警官急忙趕去協助穿著斗篷的高挑金髮女郎，她正要穿越一輛卡車正要衝下來的街口。

p. 78-79 索匹往東邊一條施工中的街道走去，憤怒地將傘丟在路邊坑洞中，他詛咒那些戴頭盔手拿警棍的傢伙，他多麼想落入他們手中呀！但他們似乎當他是至高無上、完全不犯錯的。

最後他到達往西邊的道路，那裡清靜多了。他沿著街道往麥迪遜廣場方向走去，儘管他的住所只是在廣場中的長椅上，他還是能發自本能地找到回家的路。

在一異常安靜的轉角處，索匹停下腳步，那兒有一座古老卻愜意的老舊教堂。他透過紫羅蘭色的窗戶看進去，柔和的燈光下有一位風琴手正演奏著動人的音符，他可能是在為下星期的彌撒做練習吧。美妙樂聲傳入索匹耳裡，引他停駐在教堂門外的鐵欄邊。

p. 80–81　月亮皎潔靜謐地高掛在天邊，車輛與行人稀稀落落，屋頂下麻雀睏倦地啾叫著，片刻間看起來就像是鄉間的院落。風琴手彈奏的彌撒曲，讓索匹陷入靜默中，在他年少時，他對這首曲子是很熟的。喔……昔日美好的時光，那時他擁有慈愛的父母、摯友、遠大的志向和又新又乾淨的衣服。

索匹疲倦而開放的心境，搭配上在教堂外頭所歷經的感受，突然使他的內心產生了美好的改變。

他突然一個震驚，體認到自己的人生竟變得如此悽慘，盡是墮落、無意義的欲求、無望的希望和麻木不仁，這是死路一條。他活著，就僅為了基本需求。在他孤獨悲慘的日子裡，沒有更遠大的目標，像是愛情、志向，或是想要功成名就的心。

p. 82–83　這一刻，這一種嶄新的心情，帶給了他新的想法。他突然起了一個強烈的念頭，驅使他想對抗自己的悲慘命運。他要脫離無家可歸的情況，好好振作起來，他要戰勝長久擄獲著他的惡魔；時間還夠，他還算年輕；他記住那些過去所擁有的夢想，他要不屈不撓地追尋。

那些莊嚴而甜蜜的音符，在他體內引起波濤。明天，他就要到鬧區去找份工作，曾經有一位皮草進口商願意雇用他當司機呢！他會找到那位先生，並且求得此職位。有一天他，會成為全球的大人物，他會……

怎麼好像有人把手放在臂膀上？他快速地環視四周，卻看見一個警官的寬闊臉龐。警察問他：「你在這裡做什麼？」

「沒什麼。」索匹回答。

「那麼走吧，你深夜遊蕩，被逮捕了。」警察說。

隔天上午，警局法庭中法官宣判：「在布萊克威爾斯島上，服刑三個月。」

了解故事背景：歐・亨利的人生

p. 86-87　歐・亨利本名為威廉希尼波特，出生在美國北卡羅來納州的格林斯堡市。十五歲時，搬到德州居住，並在一家藥局工作，之後轉職到牧場。

他是個熱中於閱讀的狂熱分子，受此影響，他試圖要辦雜誌，然而不久後卻失敗了。後來，他在德州這大城市的《休斯頓報》找到一份採訪記者的工作。

他婚後育有一女，之後卻因盜用報社公款，而被送進了俄亥俄州監獄。他的罪行引起許多爭議，服刑期間為了扶養家庭，開始了短篇故事寫作。

出獄後，他將姓名改為歐・亨利，並搬到紐約居住了八年之久。這段時間，他創作百來個短篇故事，大部分靈感取自於居住過或拜訪的地方。

故事多以地區環境背景作區隔，像是南方、西部、拉丁美洲或紐約，但他最有名的的短篇故事，還是以描述紐約人們歷經諷刺、意外波折後，造化弄人的結局為主，這些出人意料的結局，說明了生命中有許多不確定性會誘發人性中的善與惡。

二十年後

[第一章] 二十年的約定

p. 90-91　一位警官威嚴地在大街上巡視，看樣子他的威嚴並非刻意擺架子，只是慣於如此，因為附近沒什麼人。這時正好晚上十點，帶有些許水氣的陣陣寒風，使得人人都留在家中。

他逐一確認門是上鎖的，像是位武術大師般地轉動著警棍。他不時地轉過身，以警戒的眼神掃視大街。他高大的體型與自信的步伐，描繪出好一幅和平守護者的景象。

他負責的這一帶，商家都特別早打烊，偶爾會瞧見酒館或是全日營業店家燈火通明，但多數店家老闆早就在好個小時前就回家了。

p. 92–93　大約巡視完半個街區，他忽然放慢腳步。在五金行昏暗的門口處，有個人倚在那裡，嘴上叼著未點燃的雪茄。警察走到他身旁，遊蕩者立即說道：「長官，沒事的。」他很確信地繼續說：「我在等一位朋友，我們在二十年前約好了。聽起來有點荒謬吧？如果你想確定一切都沒有問題，那麼我會向你說明。現在的這家五金行，在以前是一家叫做『老喬布萊迪餐坊』的店。」

　　「它五年前被拆掉了。」警察說。

　　男子劃火柴將雪茄點燃，火光下是一張蒼白、右眉頭有著疤痕卻眼神銳利的方臉，在他的領巾上，別著一個鑽石飾針。

p. 94–95　「二十年前的今晚，我和吉米威爾斯在老喬布萊迪餐坊用餐，他是我最要好的兄弟，也是世界上最棒的人。我們一起在紐約長大，那年我十八歲，他二十歲，像親兄弟一樣。那時我隔天就要到西部打拼江山，而吉米是沒法離開紐約的人，他以為那是世界上僅有的地方。

　那晚我們倆約定好，不管彼此發展如何，或距離多遠，二十年後都要在這裡碰面。無論結果好壞，二十年內各自努力賺錢。」

　　「聽起來很有趣，你們似乎很久沒有碰頭了，你離開後，難道都沒有他的消息？」警察問。

p. 96–97　男子說：「有一陣子我們時常通信，但大概一兩年後就失去聯絡了。你知道的嘛，西部這麼大，我又居無定所。如果吉米還活著，一定會來和我會合的，他是世間少有的摯友，一定不會忘記的。我遠從千里來到這家店的門口，能見上老友一面，很值得了。」他邊說，邊掏出一只昂貴的錶，在街燈昏暗光線下，閃耀出鑽石的光芒。

他說：「再三分鐘就十點了，這是二十年前在餐廳前告別彼此的時間。」

警察問：「你在西部混得不錯吧？」

「沒錯！我希望吉米有我一半成功，他人不錯，就是懶了點。紐約會使人怠惰，該要把他放到西部去磨練磨練。」

p. 98–99　警察轉動棍子，移動了幾步，說道：「我該走了，希望你朋友會平安地出現。要是他沒準時出現，你會離開嗎？」

「不會！至少要等上半小時，吉米如果活著，他就會出現！長官，再見啦。」

「晚安了，先生。」警察回答後，走往街上巡察門口。

天開始落下微微細雨，冷風呼嘯吹過，路上行人紛紛豎起領口，手插口袋，神情陰鬱快步地靜靜走過。而在五金行的門口處，有一個人，不管看起來如何荒謬，他為了兒時的承諾，千里迢迢趕來，仍在那裡抽著雪茄，等待著。

p. 100–101　約過了二十分鐘，有一個高大、身著大衣立起領口的男人，急急忙忙地從對街朝等待者走來，疑惑地問：「你是鮑伯嗎？」

「是吉米威爾斯嗎？」門前等待的人大聲說。

「太不可思議了！」剛到的男人驚呼著，牽起對方的兩隻手，說道：「是信守承諾的鮑伯啊！若你還活著，我就知道我們會再見面。哇，哇，哇，已經二十年了，真希望餐廳還在，我們就能再一起用餐。老傢伙，你在西部過得可好？」

「好極了，我賺到所有想要的東西。吉米，你變好多喔，我記得你以前沒這麼高，比我記憶中還高上不少呢。」

140

「我二十歲以後又長高了一些。」

p. 102–103 「吉米，在紐約過得如何？」

「普普通通囉，在政府機關單位做事。好了啦，鮑伯，我帶你去一個我知道的地方，然後好好聊聊那些往日時光。」

兩個人互挽臂膀，在街上走著，西部人開始談論豐功偉業，為自己事業的成功感到興奮；而隱藏於外套下的人則是饒富興味地聽著。

轉角處有家電燈亮著的藥房，走過光線處時，他們彼此互看了一眼，那個西部來的人忽然停下腳步、甩開他的手。

「你不是吉米威爾斯。」他厲聲說：「二十年很長，但不足以讓一個人的鼻子，由又薄又長，變得又短又寬。」

p. 104–105 「可是，有時它會讓好人變成壞人。」高大的男人接著說：「十分鐘前，你就已經被捕了，老奸鮑伯。芝加哥警方知道你會來紐約，想跟你聊聊。回警局前，有人要我將紙條交給你，就在這櫥窗外讀吧，是威爾斯警官給的。」

鮑伯鎮靜地打開字條，他的手在閱讀時開始顫抖。這是一張短短的字條，上面寫著：

鮑伯：

我準時在約定的地方出現了。當你點燃火柴，要抽雪茄時，我看見的是張芝加哥通緝要犯的臉龐。但我無法親自下手，所以找了一個便衣警察來完成任務。

吉米

Answers

P. 30

(A) ① T ② F ③ F ④ F

(B) ① sketching ② looking ③ getting well
④ whistling ⑤ counting

P. 31

(C) ① (c) ② (a)

(D) ① unseen ② touching ③ climbed
④ breath ⑤ blown

P. 46

(A) ① (b) ② (c)

(B) ① - C ② - D ③ - A ④ - B

P. 47

(C) ① T ② T ③ F ④ F ⑤ F

(D) ① - D ② - E ③ - B ④ - A ⑤ - C

P. 66

(A) ① uneasily ② touching ③ suspiciously
④ Quietly

(B) ① - B ② - D ③ - A ④ - E ⑤ - C

P. 67

(C) ① F ② T ③ F ④ T

(D) ① → ⑤ → ④ → ③ → ②

P. 84 **A** ① - Ⓓ ② - Ⓔ ③ - Ⓑ ④ - Ⓒ ⑤ - Ⓐ

B ① vicious ② ambitious ③ gloomy
④ aggressive

P. 85 **C** ① (a) ② (b)

D ① leaned against the wall of the building
② threw the umbrella into an open hole
③ he realized how terrible his life had become

P. 106 **A** ① (a) ② (b)

B ① note ② fortune ③ jewelry ④ club

P. 120 **A** ① A homeless person in New York City → Ⓒ
② An artist who gave up on living → Ⓑ
③ A failed artist who dreamed of painting
a wonderful work. → Ⓐ
④ A criminal wanted by the Chicago Police
Department → Ⓓ

B ① What was Soapy finally arrested for? (b)
② What was the doctor's final advice for Sue? (a)

P. 121 **C** ① Soapy realized he should change his life. (T)
② Both Jimmy and Bob kept their appointment. (T)
③ Johnsy and Sue were natives of New York City. (F)
④ Behrman sacrificed his life so that Johnsy would
not die. (T)

D ① lived, on ② planned, to
③ change, ways ④ recognize, uniformed
⑤ white, statue ⑥ cried, bitterly

歐‧亨利短篇小說【二版】
Short Stories of O. Henry

作者 _ 歐‧亨利
　　　（O. Henry）

改寫 _ Brian J. Stuart

插圖 _ Kim Hyeo-Jeong

翻譯／編輯 _ 謝雅婷

作者／故事簡介翻譯 _ 王采翎

校對 _ 王采翎

封面設計 _ 林書玉

排版 _ 葳豐／林書玉

製程管理 _ 洪巧玲

發行人 _ 周均亮

出版者 _ 寂天文化事業股份有限公司

電話 _ +886-2-2365-9739

傳真 _ +886-2-2365-9835

網址 _ www.icosmos.com.tw

讀者服務 _ onlineservice@icosmos.com.tw

出版日期 _ 2019年8月 二版一刷（250201）

郵撥帳號 _ 1998620-0 寂天文化事業股份有限公司

國家圖書館出版品預行編目資料

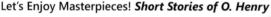

歐．亨利短篇小說 / O. Henry 原著；Brian J.
Stuart 改編；謝雅婷翻譯. -- 二版. -- [臺北市]：
寂天文化, 2019.08
　　面；　公分
中英對照
ISBN 978-986-318-823-0 (25K 平裝附光碟片)

1. 英語 2. 讀本

805.18　　　　　　　　　　　　108012302